We hope you enjoy th
Please return or rene
You can renew it at **www.norfolk.gov.uk/libraries**
or by using our free library app. Otherwise you can
phone **0344 800 8020** - please have your library
card and pin ready.
You can sign up for email reminders too.

WITHDRAWN

NORFOLK COUNTY COUNCIL
LIBRARY AND INFORMATION SERVICE

NORFOLK ITEM

3 0129 08546 0823

JAMIE McFLAIR

VS THE

BOYBAND GENERATOR

JAMIE McFLAIR VS THE BOYBAND GENERATOR

LUKE & SEAN
FRANKS   THORNE

ILLUSTRATED BY DAVIDE ORTU

HODDER

HODDER CHILDREN'S BOOKS

First published in Great Britain in 2021 by Hodder and Stoughton

1 3 5 7 9 10 8 6 4 2

Text copyright © Luke Franks & Sean Thorne, 2021
Illustrations copyright © Davide Ortu, 2021

The moral rights of the authors and illustrator have been asserted.

All characters and events in this publication, other than those clearly
in the public domain, are fictitious and any resemblance to
real persons, living or dead, is purely coincidental.

All rights reserved.
No part of this publication may be reproduced, stored in
a retrieval system, or transmitted, in any form or by any means, without
the prior permission in writing of the publisher, nor be otherwise circulated
in any form of binding or cover other than that in which it is published
and without a similar condition including this condition being
imposed on the subsequent purchaser.

A CIP catalogue record for this book
is available from the British Library.

ISBN 978 1 444 95602 3

Printed and bound in Great Britain by
CPI Group (UK) Ltd, Croydon CR0 4YY

The paper and board used in this book
are made from wood from responsible sources.

Hodder Children's Books
An imprint of
Hachette Children's Group
Part of Hodder and Stoughton
Carmelite House
50 Victoria Embankment
London EC4Y 0DZ

An Hachette UK Company
www.hachette.co.uk

www.hachettechildrens.co.uk

To Cel, Ju & Liam; Chris, Katie & David
S.T.

To Mike, Anne, Jonny and Gaby
L.F.

To Goose the Dog & Casey Cody Johnson
S.T. & L.F.

CHAPTER 1
BARRY BIGTIME

Barry Bigtime zoomed down the hall of his chateau in his finest puce tailcoat, lilac pantaloons and a thin grey scarf. His bare chest was puffed out like an emperor penguin's. His hair was slicked back so severely that it forced his eyebrows into permanent surprised mode. **HE LOOKED ABSURD.**

It was a big day for Barry. Important men were coming over to tell him how well he was doing at life, which he always loved.

Barry's guests were due to arrive any minute. Because his chateau was so **OUTRAGEOUSLY LARGE**, Barry had to travel through it in a bright pink golf cart to have any chance of reaching the front door in time.

As he sped past expensive sculptured tributes to his past boyband creations, he spotted the rapidly approaching figure of his private chef, Fabio.

One of Barry's favourite things to do was drive at full speed towards his housekeeping staff, changing direction at the last minute to miss them by inches but **SCARE THEM HALF TO DEATH.**

This was a particularly close call. Fabio heard the cart just in time and dived to his left at the very last second, crashing into a bronze statue of Proudy from Baezone, Barry's finest boyband creation. Barry screeched to a halt.

'I don't pay you to lay around on the job, Fabio,' sneered Barry. **'What are you feeding me today?'**

'Deep-fried penguin wings in a Jurassic broth made with real dinosaur fossils like you requested, sir,' mumbled Fabio, using the bronze shoulders of Proudy to get to his feet.

'Don't forget the lavender-infused water,' barked Barry.

Barry had been drinking lavender-infused water for the past month because it was supposed to make his farts smell like a meadow. He had been inviting all his friends over to show off his new sweet-smelling farts but when the time came for him to pass gas, it just smelt like **A NORMAL FART**. However, because Barry is rich, important and powerful, all the guests had to laugh and call him a legend despite the hot stench burning their nostrils.

'Of course, sir,' said Fabio with a bow. 'I'll start infusing the water right away.'

Barry nodded and sped away down the corridor in a flash of pinks and purples.

Barry Bigtime's chateau was built on the edge of his hometown of Crudwell. *Château*, by the way, is the French word for 'castle', but things sound more fancy in French so sometimes posh people use that word.

Barry liked making things sound more extravagant than they were. His real name was Glen Jones, but in show business, if you have a normal name like yours or ours, you choose a better one to seem more exciting.

Barry cruised into the chateau foyer and screeched to a halt inches away from one of the gardeners, who couldn't have been a day younger than seventy-five. The old man turned, yelped and fell head over heels into a fountain. He sat, stunned, in the shallow murky water as a bronze statue of Barry tinkled on his crinkly bald head.

Right on time the doorbell chimed, to the tune of Baezone's first hit single, 'Breaktime Girlfriend'.

Barry got out of the golf cart, howling with laughter at the gardener and strutted to the front door. He flung it open to see three nervous, smart-looking men on his doorstep.

'Gentlemen! So great to see you. Glad you could make it all the way to this miserable little town!'

'Barry Bigtime! King of the Boybands!' yelled a short man named Winston. He had a big nose, an auburn moustache and wore a beige suit that looked like a scarily tight squeeze. He tipped his matching cowboy hat at Barry.

'Winston, my round friend, such a delight to see you,' said Barry, who was too rich for manners.

'Gee, Barry. This is some way from the big city,' said Winston, who was trying to hide his nervousness with chatter. 'You must like something out here to have withstood the hankerin' to head to Hollywood, huh?'

Barry was born and raised in Crudwell. He'd never been popular. When he became **'KING OF THE BOYBANDS'** he'd used his millions to buy up acres of cherished parkland and built his chateau overlooking the rest of the town.

'I hate this town, Winston, and everyone who lives here,' said Barry, who looked like he could smell sewage. 'But it gives me joy to know that the same people who doubted me, now look at my gorgeous chateau with faces full of envy. Besides, I don't keep you around for your real estate advice – I need you to keep *The Big Time*'s television ratings at their lofty levels now that the new season has started.' Barry patted the short man on the head like he was a good dog, but Winston looked hot and bothered.

Barry turned to the second man. He was tall and thin, balancing circular spectacles on a nose that was as wonky as his hair was straight.

'Hector Macaulay!' bellowed Barry. He gave Hector a strong slap on the back and the man looked like he was about to shatter from the impact. Hector had the look of a man who was being sent into the Colosseum to fight lions.

'Good morning, Barry,' he said. He made a good effort to sound calm but a bead of sweat betrayed him by sliding down his forehead.

'You financial types are always so dry,' scoffed Barry. 'Looking after my money is the easiest job in the world, Macaulay! **Get a smile on your face,** I can't bear to look at you.'

Barry turned to the third man. His hair was thinning on the crown but long, silk-like strands hung past his shoulders. His ruddy skin was the same colour as a hot dog sausage. He wore a baby blue suit, an open shirt and his weathered old face looked like it had seen a lot of good times. It did not look like it was going to see any good times today, though.

'Marcos Paul!' shouted Barry unnecessarily, as Marcos was only inches from his face.

'Hello, Barry,' muttered Marcos hesitantly. 'H-how is it going my man? M-m-my dude?'

'What on earth is wrong with you?' said Barry. 'You've just come back from managing a mega-tour with Baezone and The Fenton Dogz. Did you have a little too much fun out there?'

Marcos gave a nervous chuckle and a shrug.

Barry smiled. He was used to people being nervous in his presence. **HE WAS BARRY BIGTIME!** The most powerful person in the music industry. He got lost in a daydream about how lucky other people must feel to be breathing the same air particles as him. The other men waited patiently on the doorstep as Barry's eyes glazed over, their faces in pain from exchanging too many awkward smiles.

'Come on in.'

CHAPTER 2
SINK OR SWIM

'**We're here!**' yelled Barry as the golf cart screeched to a halt. A housekeeper who hadn't been quick enough to leap out of the way rolled off the front of the cart to the floor with a splat. Barry stepped over them as if they were a dog dropping.

The men followed Barry into the largest room in the chateau. The floors were made from shiny marble and the ceiling was high and grand. In front of them was a large swimming pool in the shape of Barry's head. The pool flooring was a terrifying mosaic of Barry's face made from various precious stones.

Winston's head swivelled, searching for regular meeting items like tables and chairs, but found nothing except for a range of inflatable animals.

'Gee, Barry . . . Uh . . . Are we goin' swimmin' or are we havin' a meetin'?'

Barry stripped off his lilac tailcoat, dropped his pantaloons and flung his scarf into the air, which daintily landed on Marcos's balding head. He stood **PROUDLY** in a little pair of pink Speedos.

'We're having the meeting in the pool today. See if that can't put a smile on your stupid faces.'

'Barry, sorry,' whimpered Hector, 'but I don't have any, uh . . . stuff. For swimming.'

Do you know those times at school when a grown-up has forgotten to pack your PE kit and you have a terrible realisation that you may have to borrow old, stinky kit from lost property? This was very much the feeling of these three men.

'Stuff will be provided for all three of you.'

Barry ordered them to change. They returned and he surveyed them from the pool, leaning on his side, head on hand, in a giant inflatable clam.

Winston now wore a tiny, flesh-coloured pair of trunks that were so small you could barely tell he was wearing anything at all. It was a haunting sight and we're sorry that we have to describe it to you.

Hector was wearing a bright red pair of shorts that were far too big. He desperately clutched his £5,000 laptop with one hand while stopping his trunks from falling down with the other.

Marcos was wearing a ladies' swimming costume that was decorated with crabs, lobsters and other crustaceans, while holding on to a leather-bound folder of important-looking documents.

'Fetch an inflatable, get yourselves in here and tell me how great I am!' yelled Barry.

Hector chose a magnificent inflatable unicorn. He tucked his laptop into the elastic of his trunks, wrapped a spindly arm around the beast's neck and took to the water with the trembling grace of a baby giraffe. Winston chose a large inflatable dolphin that was sporting a rather fetching sailor's hat. Winston, who couldn't swim and was terrified of water, clung to the dolphin for dear life as he entered the pool. Marcos, who had been to his fair share of pool parties in his time, slid gracefully into the water on the back of a pink flamingo.

Barry looked around, satisfied. 'Now, start lavishing me with praise. Hector!' he yelled. **'How great are the Big Time finances?'**

Hector delicately and carefully fumbled with his laptop while trying to stay balanced on his unicorn.

'So . . . Mr Bigtime . . . I've put together a graph . . . of . . . your financial balance for the year . . .' Hector looked close to tears. He slowly turned the laptop around and showed Barry a graph. The graph was a long red line that looked like a sad worm with its tail in the air, burying its head deep underground. Worms with their heads in the ground are not good news in graph land.

Barry's eyes narrowed **DANGEROUSLY**. He paddled the inflatable clam slowly towards Hector who was trembling so hard it looked like his unicorn was trying to win a dance-off with itself.

'This doesn't look good,' snarled Barry.

Hector gulped. 'After the failures of the Barry Big Time Burgers, the closure of Barryland, and the legal costs from last year which we don't talk about . . . You owe the bank . . . a considerable amount of money.'

Barry started turning pink.

'If the next boyband you create isn't as big . . . if not *bigger* than Baezone ever were, by Christmas . . . then you could lose the chateau, the TV studio, the— **AHHHH!'**

There was a pop as Barry pulled the plug on Hector's inflatable unicorn. With a sad hiss, the unicorn's horn began to flop and then its body collapsed. Hector desperately tried to keep his laptop above water and stop his trunks from abandoning him as the unicorn sank into the depths of Barry Bigtime's pool.

Barry's eyes flashed towards Marcos. **'How has this happened?!** Baezone and The Fenton Dogz were on a mega-tour!'

'The sales were, um, disappointing,' stammered Marcos. 'Baezone hype has been diminishing for several years now, Barry, surely you've seen that? And all our other boybands have just never come close to their success. We're trying with The Fenton Dogz but unfortunately they're just a bit, you know . . .' Marcos trailed off, trying to think of a nice word. 'Average.'

Barry looked at Winston, who looked like he wanted to paddle on his inflatable dolphin back across the Atlantic. 'What about *The Big Time*'s TV ratings?'

'Gee, Barry, I don't know what to tell ya,' muttered Winston.

We'll help Winston out here: *The Big Time* ratings

stank. It used to be the biggest TV show in the world. Hopeful bands and musicians would queue for hours to audition to appear on *The Big Time* live shows. The best ones would head to *The Big Time* Grand Final, singing to win a spot at the **WORLD MUSIC FESTIVAL, THE MOST PRESTIGIOUS EVENT IN WORLD MUSIC.** (Ugh, we sound like the advert.) Anyway, the main problem here is that Barry Bigtime would always fix the voting in the final, so boybands he created always won.

'Ya see, the networks are unhappy with the ratings this year . . . It's like nobody's interested in TV singin' talent shows any more, you know? Also, the World Music Festival have been unhappy with the calibre of contestants . . .' Winston looked everywhere but at Barry. 'They're thinkin' of withdrawin' their offer of givin' the show winners a spot at the festival. They're sayin' that the acts are all the same, and a little old-fashioned – they'd prefer to give the prize to one of those big YouTube bands, or . . . **OH COME ON, BARRY!'**

The Y-word had tipped Barry over the edge. He paddled towards Winston, who had neither the grace nor guile to avoid the incoming clam. Barry grabbed the inflatable dolphin's sailor hat and tore it from its head. Air rushed out and the hatless dolphin disappeared into the pool.

Barry turned his clam towards Marcos, who, despite the carnage, was showing as much composure as possible for a man sitting on an inflatable flamingo in a crustacean-emblazoned swimming costume.

'Look, Barry, I know you hate YouTube bands,' began Marcos.

'Amateurs!' spat Barry. 'I choose who becomes successful in this industry, Marcos. Who do these little maggots think they are, trying to get famous on their own, in my world? I own it. *Me!'*

Marcos put on his most soothing voice. 'The world is changing, dude! Why don't you just think about giving the prize to someone other than your bands?

Invite one of these up-and-coming Internet bands to give it a shot? If they're good, it could boost ratings and keep the World Music Festival happy?' Marcos pulled a sheet of paper from his leather-bound file and handed it to Barry.

'A few of the music team and I have put together a list of up-and-coming bands causing a splash on YouTube.'

Barry glared at the list of young musicians who felt they could make their own way in the music industry on raw talent alone and without his brilliance. Barry jabbed at the first band name on the list with his finger.

'BNA? What does that stand for?'

Marcos shrugged. At this moment, he thought it could stand for 'Barry's Not Amused'.

'Oh, Barry, BNA are some real talented fellas. A little under the radar now, but the BNAniacs are a rabid fan base.' He paused. 'We did put some feelers out, but they said *The Big Time* may not be for them. But—'

'I'm sorry,' Barry interrupted, the intensity of his sploshing increasing. 'This BNA think they're too

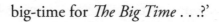

big-time for *The Big Time* . . .?'

Marcos looked Barry dead in the eyes. He knew what was coming. He said a quiet goodbye to the flamingo as with a loud **POP** and a **HISS** the flamingo's once-proud neck crumpled. The cold pool water rose above the crabs and lobsters of his swimwear and swallowed the file of Internet boybands. As he splashed, the inflatable clamshell loomed over him, Barry's head in the centre like an evil pearl.

'I want all of you to listen to me. Winston, Marcos, Hector. You get this BNA to appear on *The Big Time* tomorrow. I don't care what it takes or what you have to promise them. You get them to come to the studio and we'll see if they're too big-time for *The Big Time*.'

'But the auditions are over! Week Three of the live shows is tomorrow night!' spluttered Marcos.

'Well, I'll just invent a brand new special fast-pass wildcard rule. **It's my show, you idiot, we can do whatever we want!**' Barry yelled, splashing more water in Marcos's open mouth. 'If BNA are for whatever reason not on *The Big Time* stage tomorrow night, all three of you will be in a very different pool with some very different creatures, none of which will be inflatable.'

With that he stormed out of the pool, leaving the three men thrashing around after the worst tell-Barry-how-good-he-is-at-life day ever.

Barry **SQUELCHED,** still sopping wet, to the golf cart, fired up the engine and zipped down the hall. He was heading to his laboratory. There was only one way to save *The Big Time*. It was time to fire up the **BOYBAND GENERATOR** once more.

CHAPTER 3

GRANDMA AND THE SMELLS

It was 6.30 a.m. on Saturday morning when Jamie McFlair was violently awoken by the screeching alarm of a tablet dispenser.

We all know this is an unusual wake-up call for an eleven-year-old, but then again not many eleven-year-olds share a bedroom with their grandma.

Jamie's nose began filling with the scent of Grandma's ointments, perfumes and other old lady smells as the shrieking of the tablet dispenser continued. Jamie sat up, rubbed away her eye bogies and pulled a tangle of red hair from her face. Grandma was still blissfully asleep.

'How are you not awake?' Jamie said loudly, exasperated.

Still no movement from Grandma. **(SHE'S NOT DEAD, BY THE WAY.)**

Sharing a room with your grandma is as rubbish as you can imagine. If you've ever disliked sharing a bedroom with your brother or sister, Jamie McFlair would assure you that it could be loads worse. At least your brother or sister doesn't make everything smell like the olden days.

Must. Deal. With. That. Noise . . . Getting out of bed was tricky for Jamie as Grandma parked her mobility scooter in the small gap between their two beds.

'Here we go again,' Jamie said for the sixth time that week, grabbing her phone, switching on the torch and clambering on to the mobility scooter. With one foot on the frame of her elderly room mate's bed and the other on the saddle of the scooter, she reached across to the shelf above Grandma's snoring head. Surrounded by a smug-looking troupe of china pigs, the tablet dispenser continued to **YELP** at Jamie. 'This much noise in the morning should be illegal,' she muttered.

The tray with Grandma's medicine stuck out like a tongue. Jamie scooped the five tablets into her hand and pushed the tray back into the dispenser with her elbow, which brought the noisy ordeal to an end. Jamie took a moment to savour the silence. Part one of her **DAILY MISSION** was complete. Jamie awarded herself fifty bonus points for resisting the temptation to smash one of the china pigs.

She carefully climbed on to the floor, placing a foot either side of the front left wheel of the mobility scooter.

'Grandma . . .' Jamie whispered, trying her hardest not to startle the old prune. She shone her phone light on to the wrinkly face. It wasn't the most flattering of lighting. Grandma's mouth hung open, showing one lonely tooth in a mouth full of gum.

After several attempts, Grandma was still out cold. Jamie was left with one final option. She reached over and tooted the horn of the mobility scooter. After around four and a half seconds of the scooter's loud **MEEEEEEP!** (which is actually a long time if you count it in your head), Grandma's eyes snapped open and she sat bolt upright like someone had zapped life into Frankenstein's monster. She **SCREAMED** and **FARTED**. Jamie didn't know whether to cover her nose or ears.

'What on earth is all this ruckus, Reginald? Is that you?' Grandma's eyes blinked in the gleam of Jamie's phone light.

'I'm not Reginald, Grandma. It's Jamie.'

'Don't play games, Reginald! **You know you're on thin ice with me, sunshine!'** snapped Grandma.

Jamie flicked the switch on the bedroom wall, flooding the room with light. She looked at Grandma. Her white, patchy hair made her look like someone had tried to glue clumps of cotton wool on to a crinkly old potato.

'Oh, Jamie! It's you!' said Grandma, her face brightening. 'I thought you were an ex-husband of mine, Reginald Whittaker! He's been dead for five years, bless his soul. He always said he'd haunt me.' Grandma yawned, stretched and **FARTED AGAIN**.

'I'm awfully glad it's you but what are you doing in my room at this ridiculous hour?'

'It's my room too, Grandma,' sighed Jamie, slightly nervous at the idea of a ghost showing up in her bedroom, though she already felt haunted by the ghosts of Grandma's bottom. 'I'm here for the same reason I always wake you up – to give you your medicine.'

The old lady was looking around the room as if she'd woken up in it for the very first time. Jamie knew that Grandma's brain was like one of those old computers that took ages to start up.

When Grandma first moved in, to help her settle, Jamie's mum had redecorated the old lady's side of the room. As I'm sure you've guessed, Grandma's half of the room was **UGLY**. In all capital letters, **bold and underlined**. The wallpaper was pink and purple stripes while the carpet was apple green, and a signed, framed photo of Baezone hung from the wall.

Jamie's side of the room was wallpapered with posters of her favourite YouTubers, a band called **BNA**. The majority of posters featured Scott. More on Scott later. You can't really think about Scott when looking at Grandma.

'You're a good girl,' said Grandma. 'Could you be a gentle bear and bring my special little boy over for a morning snuggle?' Her bony finger pointed to the corner of the bedroom, where a fat pig snoozed in a dog basket.

Oh yes, that's right. We hadn't mentioned the pig yet, had we? We were distracted by the offensive noises and smells. But yes, if the horrors of sharing a bedroom with an 88-year-old lady weren't enough, Jamie's other unwanted roommate was a **BAD-TEMPERED, POT-BELLIED PIG.**

Back when Sheamus was a piglet, he had been given to Grandma as an eightieth birthday present by her son, who insisted he was one of those micropigs that would never grow bigger than a shoebox. It turned out Sheamus was **NOT** a micropig, but more of a **JUMBOPIG** who kept growing and growing and could barely fit in the dog basket.

While Grandma swallowed her pills, Jamie hoisted Sheamus out of his basket, with great difficulty. He was, as we said, a right little chunkster.

Sheamus was less than thrilled about his

early-morning journey and started oinking and wriggling. Times like this made Jamie wish that Sheamus would be recruited for a one-way mission to space. She dropped the pig into Grandma's arms.

Jamie was cursed with being a good person. She firmly believed that people who did and thought nice things would have happier endings than those who thought and did cruel things. Scott from BNA had taught her that. Jamie looked at Grandma snuggling Sheamus. She felt bad that she wished Sheamus was a space pig because she knew he made Grandma happy.

JAMIE'S WORK HERE WAS DONE.

CHAPTER 4
A SHOT AT *THE BIG TIME*

Jamie sleepily stumbled into the living room. It was still dark as the autumnal sun hadn't bothered to show up yet, but Jamie could just make out the small, snoozing figure of Buttons the pug. His gurgly snores rose from his bundle of old blankets, his new spot since Sheamus had stolen his basket. Jamie crouched down by the pug, stroking his head. 'One day I'm going to get you out of here,' said Jamie. 'I'm going to get us a big house. You, me, Mum . . .'

And Grandma, chimed in Jamie's conscience. *We can't leave Grandma all by herself.*

'The new house will be so big we can have our OWN mega-big rooms. It'll be even bigger and nicer than stupid, horrible, awful Barry Bigtime's mansion or "gateau" or whatever he calls it. It'll be the coolest place in Crudwell; all my friends would live with us too and even BNA would be actual friends with us and play gigs in the living room.'

She wished crazy daydreams were a topic in her exams this year. She'd definitely get **FULL MARKS**. She looked at her tired, freckly face in the reflection of her tablet screen. With that thought firmly in her mind, she switched it on.

BNA had been Jamie's life ever since Daisy had introduced them to her in Year 4. Scott was her favourite. You might guess that he was the lead singer, but you'd be *wrong*. He played bass. He was technically the least popular of the band because he had fewer Twitter followers than everyone else but Jamie didn't care. Last year, Scott liked Jamie's 'Happy 14th Birthday' tweet, which she printed out, framed and hung above her bed.

Scott was the reason Jamie had started her own YouTube channel, and gave her hope that one day she would get famous enough to move her family away from Crudwell and to somewhere, anywhere better. But you don't need us to tell you that wasn't going to happen with her nine subscribers and thirty-two minutes of watch time. *Must stick to an upload schedule*, she thought.

Scott had it way worse than Jamie. Before he became a famous YouTuber, Scott had no money, no dad, had escaped a war and still managed to become a successful musician. Jamie's life was similar except her war was with her grandma's routine and Tobias Merryweather . . .

More on Tobias later, as Jamie had just noticed a **NEW VIDEO** notification from BNA's channel, titled:

EXCITING ANNOUNCEMENT

Her face flicked between the one eyebrow raised emoji and the thinking face emoji several times. She never got caught out by a BNA announcement. She was the president of the BNAniacs Fan Society, she was an admin to four different Twitter and Instagram fan accounts, and she'd even learnt how to Facebook from her mum. Technically, Jamie wasn't old enough to use social media, but her **MUM WAS COOL ABOUT IT** as long as she checked in with her now and again.

Jamie had spent two summers learning advanced coding so that she could build a social network of BNA fans called BNAspace. Jamie's prize possession was a pair of **SPY-MAN GLASSES** that allowed her to record and stream BNA gigs in 4K while looking *super* smart. This meant people on BNAspace who couldn't always make it to gigs got to watch the show from home. The spy-man glasses were also how Mr Rogers got fired for not being accepting of all cultures and religions in RE once. Jamie was so dedicated to BNA, she always knew they were going to do things way before they posted them. How had this exciting announcement passed her by?

She tapped the video.

J, Harrison, Beck and Scott immediately appeared.

No intro sequence, thought Jamie, *that's weird . . .*

Harrison, Beck and Scott were **CRAMMED** into the back of a car, with J, who was holding up the camera, in the front passenger seat. They were all looking great by a normal person's standards, but a little jaded for BNA's.

'Hey, guys!' J said cheerily with a wave. J was the lead singer. He had dark skin, very short black hair and a cheeky grin.

'We've got some mad news for you … Do you want to tell them, Harrison? I think it's too funny.' J found **EVERYTHING** funny. He passed the camera to the back of the car.

Harrison had long brown hair, a pale face and was stockier than the rest of the group. He had a northern English twang to his voice and was squinting into the lens.

'Man, I look dreadful,' said Harrison. 'OK, you lot won't believe this. We're off t'television studio this morning! **Actual television!** People who don't live on t'Internet are going to watch us sing. How mad is that?'

'The television?' Jamie's brown eyes widened. Her boys were finally going to hit the mainstream!

Beck's perfect tangle of blonde hair and tanned baby face appeared into shot.

'I reckon it's all a wind-up!' he yelled into the camera. 'This doesn't feel right to me! I'm not having it. So let this be evidence that me, Beck Rhys, *knew all along* that this was a prank.' He disappeared out of shot with a laugh.

Scott reached across Beck and grabbed the camera from Harrison. Scott had a mop of jet-black hair, light brown skin and excellent dimples. He was a **VERY HANDSOME-LOOKING CHAP** and was always smiling.

'So basically, guys,' Scott began as Jamie beamed, 'we got a call really late last night from a TV producer. They've invited us to perform on *THE BIG TIME* . . .'

'They essentially begged for us to come on!' came J's voice from off-camera.

'We didn't even have to audition. They've given us a special fast-pass wildcard thing. We're going straight to the live shows. **It's mad!'**

'And they gave us all a special black card that gives us unlimited Chungus Chicken!' added J.

'We weren't keen to start with, but we decided it would be cool for you guys to see us on the TV, plus we could actually win a spot at the World Music Festival!' Scott took a deep breath. 'As you know from my "Draw My Life!" video, it's my lifelong dream!'

'And Harrison loves Chungus Chicken!' J chipped in.

A cheer rose from the rest of the lads in the car. 'We're performing tonight at 7 p.m. We hope you guys will support us and hopefully we can impress Barry Bigtime and win that spot at the **World Music Festival.'**

Jamie's mouth fell open. BNA were appearing on *The Big Time*? Tonight? Was this good news? It didn't feel like good news. This was an **EMERGENCY SITUATION**. It was time to take a selfie.

She held up four fingers. Pouted, raised one eyebrow, took a selfie and uploaded it to Instagram with a Valencia filter. No caption. Just one hashtag: **#FOURTHIRTY**.

She sat down and Buttons the pug crawled sleepily into her lap. They both stared at Jamie's phone **INTENTLY**, waiting for the likes.

x_JamieBNA_x

#fourthirty

Jenners likes this.
Mel likes this.
Daisy likes this.

This was the **VALENCIAN FOUR-FINGERED SALUTE.**
A secret signal between four friends. It meant one thing:

An emergency meeting had to take place that day at 4.30 p.m.

CHAPTER 5

THE BOYBAND GENERATOR

Barry's levels of **RAGE** were above average.

In fact, they'd been on a gradual incline since yesterday's pool meeting. More than once Barry's **STRESSED-OUT** brain had woken him up in the middle of the night with urgent problems. These included:

How will I afford all the loop-the-loops I'll need for my personal rollercoaster?

Will my cutlery have to be made out of silver instead of gold?

I'm hungry.

What if I have to start going to supermarkets full of stinky normal people? Will I have to drink non-chocolatey cow milk?!

Wealth is a strange beast. No matter how much you

have, your brain always wants **MORE.** Barry's current dream was to build a rollercoaster around his chateau. Not that the chateau wasn't already ridiculous enough.

Barry's chateau had **OVER FIFTY ROOMS,** including two pools, a hall for parties, his own personal pizza restaurant, a bouncy marshmallow room for calming his tantrums and some rooms that are so bizarre and integral to the story that we can't just breeze past them here. In fact, we're on our way to one of those rooms now . . .

Barry's cart once again screeched into the foyer to meet his next guests: a wealthy-looking lady with her posh-looking sons. They all **STANK OF MONEY.** These boys were going to be the next big boyband and fix all of Barry's problems . . . or so he hoped. He looked at the boys and came up with their name there and then: The Last Chance Crew. We give that name a five out of ten.

'Oh, Mr Bigtime, we are so grateful for this opportunity,' fawned the boys' mother, Mrs Badonday, nervously twiddling her curls. 'I promise you they are so talented and will not let you down, will you, boys?'

The Last Chance Crew looked at each other hesitantly.

'Answer your mother!' barked Mrs Badonday.

The boys hurriedly mumbled words of agreement. One broke into song, while the others started clumsily breakdancing. Right now they looked like The No Chance Crew. Barry closed his eyes. He'd need to work hard with this lot.

'Have you signed the confidentiality agreement?' asked Barry.

'I certainly have,' said Mrs Badonday, handing over the contract followed by a brown bag with a dollar sign on it.

'Good. So you're aware that if you breathe one word about what happens in this chateau to anyone, you're liable to be fed to an animal of my choosing? I'll give you a clue – **it will be a shark.'**

Mrs Badonday looked terrified but nodded.

'Splendid. Then follow me.'

Barry took the family to the southern wing of his chateau. They entered a library filled with old DVD boxsets and the general whiff of bad experiences. Barry walked over to a bookcase, grabbed Season 2 of a spooky comedy called *Gnome Alone* and pulled the battered box downwards. The shelves began to **RUMBLE** and shake as they moved inwards and to one side.

They stood at the entrance to Barry Bigtime's laboratory. Now you may think that his laboratory would be in a cold, spooky stone cellar. You know, the sort where lame cartoon baddies would hang out. But those laboratories are so 90s. Barry's lab was as needlessly extravagant as the rest of his mansion. The walls were an electric shade of pink, lit with pickle jars filled with Ecuadorian fireflies (the rarest and brightest of the fireflies).

The showpiece of the room made the Badonday family's eyebrows vanish into their hair. The far end of the room was taken up by ginormous glass domes. From the roof of each dome, a helmet hung by a tangle of tubes and wires. The wires, like the roots of a tree, led upwards and joined into one large pipe that spiralled like a serpent into a large effigy of **BARRY'S OWN FACE** with a wide gaping mouth.

Mrs Badonday pinched her arm to check she was definitely awake, which is such a mum thing to do.

'What the . . .' she said, which probably sums up what we're all thinking.

Barry smirked and spread his arms wide. **'Behold, the Boyband Generator!'**

It seemed impossible. It seemed unimaginable. It seemed wildly unhygienic, but we can tell you it was true. **THIS WAS BARRY'S SECRET.** (Remember, the one we mentioned on the back cover to entice you to buy this book?)

'So this is how Baezone, Shake District, The Oi Oi Ladz . . .' Mrs Badonday stuttered.

'You're smarter than you look, Mrs Gurbonbay.' Barry sneered. 'Every successful boyband in the world had been made in this machine. I know what you're thinking: yes, **I am a handsome genius.'**

What we were really thinking was maybe this technology could be put to **BETTER USE** than making boybands.

'How does it work?' asked Mrs Badonday, for the first time mildly concerned about what she'd got her children into. Not to mention she'd told her husband that she was only taking them swimming.

'Do you understand quantum mechanical synthesis?' Barry asked impatiently.

'Erm . . . No,' came Mrs Badonday's reply.

'Do you understand multi-enzyme complex DNA replication?' he continued.

'No, I don't,' she said.

'Well stop asking questions, then!' Barry snapped, his internal rage-o-meter reaching new highs as his face deepened to the shade of a ripe plum.

We can fill you in, though. Barry would take normal boys, put them under the glass domes, fill the mouth of the generator with ingredients that would be extracted and transported **MENTALLY** and **PHYSICALLY** into the new boyband. Sure, this explanation won't get you full marks in your science exam, but it will do for now.

Speaking of ingredients . . . if the Badonday family could have torn their eyes away from the generator, they would have seen hundreds of giant gumball machines around the sides of the lab. This is where Barry kept the ingredients. Things like **SKINNY JEANS, QUIFFS AND MATURE CHEDDAR CHEESE.**

Mrs Badonday gulped, but had one more important question to ask. 'Were The Fenton Dogz made here too?' After all, in the last twelve months, The Fenton Dogz had only trended worldwide twice and not for good musical reasons.

Barry put a finger on Mrs Badonday's lips and turned to the boys.

'Boys, find yourself a dome and strap

those helmets to your head. Kiss Mummy goodbye now. The next time you see her you'll be ready for **superstardom** and won't want anything more to do with her.'

The boys looked at Barry with wide eyes and did as they were told. Barry doo-bee-dooed as he began collecting ingredients, his bad temper disappearing as he thought about tonight. Getting these YouTube know-it-alls BNA to appear on *The Big Time* had been easier than he thought. It just so happened that one of the little worms had lifelong dreams of performing at the World Music Festival. Plus no one could resist a Chungus Chicken black card.

He would **DESTROY** BNA and launch this new boyband, The Last Chance Crew – his greatest creation yet! He chuckled as he imagined BNA having to follow this work of art. The boos of the crowd, the atmosphere of disappointment, the slow realisation on their faces that they weren't as good as they thought they were.

Barry went to the first towering gumball machine of boyband smiles and turned the crank. He heard a tinkle and opened the dispenser to find four very average little teeth. He frowned and turned the crank again. Out trickled another handful of mediocre-looking gnashers. A little bead of sweat oozed from Barry's big-time brow. **WHERE WERE ALL THE GOOD TEETH?!**

Next to the tooth dispenser was a white oak cabinet with handles that curled like a snail's shell. This is where the boyband hair lived. Boyband hair isn't hair like yours or ours. Boyband hair is alive and **MISCHIEVOUS.** How could something look so messy yet stay so perfect unless it was alive? Boyband hair lives on an island off the coast of Madagascar and Barry would send his minions to pluck the poor little boyband hair creatures for his supplies.

Barry flung open the doors. The shelves were empty apart from a glum-looking mop of limp hair that was slowly crawling across a shelf. Things didn't get better for Barry from there. Everywhere he looked, he was met with depleted, sub-par boyband ingredients. A tiny nervous fart **SQUEAKED** out of Barry's bottom that did not smell anything like a meadow.

How could he make a boyband without any decent

ingredients? We'll tell you this, in case you hadn't realised: Barry's main problem was that he liked himself **A LOT**, in fact more than anything else in the world. There was a nagging sensible voice in his head that said things like, *Maybe you should save some money for the future, rather than buy a solid gold statue of yourself for the garden*, or *Deep-fried penguin wings are both expensive and seriously damaging the existence of a rare species of bird*. But that voice wasn't fun, so Barry always ignored it. If he'd listened to it, it would have told him he was running low on essential boyband ingredients. And now he didn't even have enough left to make a boyband suitable for the Crudwell Donkey Derby, let alone perform at the **WORLD MUSIC FESTIVAL.**

Barry scraped together every last ingredient and dumped them into the large gaping mouth of the machine. With less than seven hours until BNA's live global **HUMILIATION,** the entirety of his boyband ingredient supplies exhausted and his desperate need to create the next big boyband, these boys truly were The Last Chance Crew. He closed his eyes, cranked the humongous lever and **HOPED FOR THE BEST.**

The domes glowed as The Last Chance Crew boys'
brains were being reprogrammed and their faces,
hairstyles and clothes rearranged. Behind the glass
domes, a series of pumping pistons sent multicoloured

liquids down **BUBBLING** tubes. Mrs Badonday's wide eyes followed the liquids' twisting and twirling as they sped round and round before being sucked into the domes. A series of cogs spun at a ferocious pace, where wires connected them to two plinths. On top of each sat a glowing purple globe. Every few seconds a **ZAP** of electricity would crackle across from one to the other and the whole machine would shake. After exactly four minutes, the bubbles began to mellow and the domes began to dim. A loud **DING!** from what sounded like the world's largest microwave indicated that the generation was complete.

The domes opened and the boys **STEPPED OUT.**

One of them immediately fell over his shoelaces, another smiled to reveal a mouth of entirely crooked teeth. One boy's hair leapt off his head, leaving him as bald as an egg.

Barry took one look at them and stormed towards the laboratory door, to the protests of Mrs Badonday.

'What have you done to my boys?' Mrs Badonday yelled. 'The *Crudwell Gazette* will hear of this!'

Barry spun around.

'You know the rules. One word to anyone and the lot of you are shark food.'

That made everyone pipe down.

Without a boyband to crush BNA's dreams and save his legacy, **BARRY NEEDED A PLAN B.**

CHAPTER 6
THE VALENCIAN FOUR-FINGERED SALUTE

Jamie was sitting in the kitchen. Her mum, Sarah, was tidying while her mum's boyfriend, Dominic, sat reading the *Crudwell Gazette*. For the first time in her life, Jamie was experiencing **AMBIVALENCE**. This is when you feel two very different emotions about one single thing. It felt like her brain was a lovely cottage of happiness with incessantly irritating inhabitants.

On the surface, it seemed great that BNA were performing on *The Big Time*. OK, maybe the show wasn't as popular as it used to be, but it was still great exposure, plus there was the chance that BNA could perform at the **WORLD MUSIC FESTIVAL,** which she knew was Scott's dream. But there wasn't anything involving *The Big Time* that ever turned out good.

Sheamus the pig **WADDLED** into the kitchen, treading unidentifiable pig muck into the freshly cleaned floor.

Jamie's mum yelled, **'Mother!** Can you keep that pig out of the kitchen please! It's filthy!' as she chased Sheamus away with a mop.

'Grandma's not in, Mum,' said Jamie. 'It's Saturday; Crudwell Rovers are at home. She's gone with Ethel and Olivia.'

'I thought they were still **BANNED** from the stadium?'

'It expired last week,' said Jamie. 'You still haven't told me why she got banned in the first place.'

'Streaking,' replied Dominic with a shudder.

'What's streaking?' asked Jamie.

'It doesn't matter,' snapped Sarah, flashing an angry glance at Dominic.

'At least Ethel won't be able to get on the pitch any more, not with her hip.'

Jamie's mum was once a skydiving and bungee jump instructor and had always secretly wanted to be a **PIRATE**. Sadly there were no suitable bungee jumping hotspots in Crudwell, nor any nearby vessels to plunder. She now also had Jamie and her own mother to look after all by herself. So her hopes and dreams had to take a backseat to the world of telesales. She often wondered how she'd got to a point in life where she was chasing a pig out of her kitchen, but didn't like to dwell on the thought too much.

Sarah's boyfriend Dominic was a reasonably pleasant but very average man. He was classic Crudwell. Dominic used to be a **DETECTIVE,** like Sherlock Holmes, but because Crudwell was so boring there was nothing to investigate. He'd had to give up his dream of being a detective and now worked in the Crudwell paper factory.

'The paper quality of the *Crudwell Gazette* has really gone downhill in the last eighteen months,' said Dominic in a sentence that was so **BORING** it's surprising every person and pig in the room didn't fall instantly asleep.

The *Crudwell Gazette* was supposed to be a newspaper but nothing ever really happened in Crudwell. The journalists usually just made stuff up to fill space. The front page read **'GOOSE ON THE LOOSE'** and pictured a shifty-looking goose. Did this goose even exist? Dominic wondered if the goose needed privately investigating, but then remembered his dreams were dead.

'Are you OK, Jamie? You look miles away,' her mum said.

'I'm fine,' said Jamie, who wouldn't learn the word 'ambivalence' until Year 8.

It was 4.29 p.m. Her Valencian Four-Fingered Salute emergency meeting was due to start any minute.

Despite the pigs, grandmas and boring boyfriends, one of the good things about Jamie's house was that everyone was always welcome to pop in and say hello. Jamie's mum liked her having friends round. When Sarah was a little girl, her nasty brother had always scared her friends away. The clock struck 4.30 and there were several **BLASTS** of the doorbell.

DING . . . DONG
DING . . . DONG
DINGDONG
DINGDONG

Jamie scampered to the front door. Squashed against the cloudy glass panes was the unmistakable face of Jenners. Jamie opened the door and Jenners gave her a big, **ROUGH** hug. Jenners was the muscle of Jamie's friendship group. She was the tallest and strongest girl in school and better than anyone else at football. She had light brown hair pulled back into a long, tight ponytail. Her facial features were close together, which gave her quite a large forehead – ideal for attacking and defending corners.

'Mate, I almost pooed my pants with literal excitement,' said Jenners in her voice that was always a touch too loud for inside conversation. 'What on earth is going on? Why are BNA on *The Big Time*? It feels so weird.'

Sarah also greeted Jenners with a big hug.

'I don't think I'll get used to you towering over me,' laughed Sarah. 'How's your mum? I hear she's thinking of getting back into the wrestling?'

'Yeah, she's back training three times a week now,' replied Jenners. 'She really thinks she can become world champion this time. I'm like, "Mum, seriously, you're in your fifties." But you know what she's like.'

'Well, if I had any money to gamble, I'd put it on your mum to be champion,' said Sarah with a sad laugh.

Jamie took Jenners into her room.

'Sorry about the smell,' said Jamie.

'It smells even more like museums and medicine than usual,' said Jenners, fanning her nose.

'You get used to it after a while,' Jamie lied, organising her best cushions on her bed.

Ten minutes later there was another ring of the doorbell.

DING . . . DONG . . .
DING . . . DONG

Jamie opened the door to see her friend Daisy, who was fashionably late as usual. Tall, with light brown skin and blonde hair, Daisy was dressed head to toe in black and was wearing a beret. She was one of those people that could wear weird things and nobody would question it because she was so cool.

Daisy had moved to Jamie, Jenners and Mel's junior school in Year 4 from the big city of Birchester. It was why Daisy was so much **COOLER** than everyone else. When she arrived at Crudwell it was like she was from a different planet. Jamie and Daisy became friends after Daisy showed her some new bands on YouTube that nobody had ever heard of before.

That was when Jamie had discovered Scott, Beck, J and Harrison, back when they only had 163 subscribers. In the next few days that number jumped up to 167 as Jenners and Mel hopped aboard the BNA train and from that day on the girls had **LOYALLY SUPPORTED** their favourite lads.

'I don't like this, guys,' Daisy said, adjusting her beret as she strutted into Jamie's room. '*The Big Time* hasn't been a thing since Year 3 – why are BNA going on it?' **SHE FROZE.** 'Oh my, the pong of this room always gets me.'

'Me too,' said Jenners, who still had the collar of her shirt over her nose.

DIDIDIDIDIDIDIDIDIDINGDONG DINGDONGDIDIDINGDONG!

The nervous prodding of Jamie's doorbell could only mean that Mel had arrived. Jamie opened the door to greet her oldest friend. Jamie and Mel had known each other since playgroup and Jamie had always been **VERY PROTECTIVE** of her sensitive little friend. Mel arched her neck and peered nervously into the hall with wide eyes.

'Don't worry, Mel. Grandma's gone to the football today.'

'Oh, that's good,' said Mel with a sigh of relief. She was terrified of old people.

Mel had her own 'style', though it attracted attention for the opposite reasons to Daisy's. Her clothes never really matched and were either too big or too small, or sometimes didn't look like proper clothes at all. Today she looked like she was about to go on safari. She was sporting a giant pair of binoculars around her neck and wearing a bright orange sun hat. She was clutching a carrier bag containing stale bread, wheat pellets and a **HONKER HORN.**

Jamie led Mel into the bedroom as the strange objects clattered in behind her. The rest of the girls looked at Mel with **CONFUSION**.

'Mel, why do you have all of this stuff?'
Jamie gently broke the silence.

'I thought we might need some of it,' Mel said, with a satisfied smile. She emptied her bag on to Jamie's bed. 'We could lure him out using these pellets. Plus, I've got this honker horn – the noise might make him think we're his friends.'

Daisy picked up the honker horn and examined it like it had once belonged to aliens. With a raised eyebrow, she passed it to Jenners, who impatiently squashed a slice of stale bread in her other fist.

Jamie stared at the items open-mouthed. 'Mel, what are you on about? Who are we honking?'

Mel peered at them over her glasses. 'Aren't we looking for the goose that's on the loose?'

SILENCE.

'It was in today's newspaper?'

More silence.

'I've got it wrong, haven't I?' Mel sighed. 'That's why I was late – I was looking for the honker horn. I knew I'd seen it around the house but I'd forgotten exactly where . . .'

Mel watched her friends' faces slowly change from confused to **AMUSED**. Jamie grinned and soon all four of them were laughing.

'Mel, it's fine,' said Jamie, putting an arm around her. 'We may need these things anyway. Sit down and have some squash and a cookie.'

Jamie sat up straight in the centre of her group of friends, in what she hoped was a businesslike pose. 'Did you see the BNA post this morning, Mel?' said Jamie.

Mel looked like she'd forgotten her homework. '*What?* No! But they only ever upload in the evening!'

'Don't you have notifications switched on?' asked Jenners.

'I'm not allowed push notifications because I share the tablet with my mum and she gets annoyed by them!'

The girls explained to Mel that BNA were going to perform on **THE BIG TIME** that evening and could win a spot at the World Music Festival.

Mel became **WHEEZY** with excitement. 'The World Music Festival. It's Scott's dream!' she spluttered in between pumps of her inhaler. 'They'll meet Barry Bigtime! Maybe he can get us to meet them?'

'He'd never let us meet them,' said Jenners darkly. 'Everyone knows **he's horrible.'**

'No offence, Jamie,' Daisy quickly added.

The three of them turned to Jamie, because Barry Bigtime, King of the Boybands, filthy rich music mogul and feared talent show judge was also . . .

'My Uncle Barry is one of the worst humans in the world,' Jamie said, never shy to share her feelings about her famous relation.

'It's his fault that Grandma lives with us. It's his fault my room smells of museums and medicine. It's his fault we live with a massive pig.' She paused. 'It's his fault we don't have any money.'

'Did he steal it from you? Should we call the police?' asked Mel, shocked. This was the first time Jamie had shared *that* much about her uncle.

'No, it happened years ago. My mum

lent him pretty much all of her money to start his music business when they were younger. He took the money and has never given it back despite the fact he's now disgustingly rich.'

'Thing is, though, Jamie, BNA are genuinely really good,' pointed out Daisy. 'They're not like the weird comedy old ladies that turn up and sing gangster rap. Barry Bigtime can't be horrible to them if everyone can see that they're amazing.' Daisy's wisdom made Jamie feel better. But she couldn't help but feel **NERVOUS** that Scott and the lads were walking into a trap.

'So what do we do?' asked Mel, still wheezy, confused yet excited.

'Uncle Barry being awful aside, this is a monumental moment in BNA history. As leaders of the BNAniac fan groups, we must assemble BNAniacs around the world for a group viewing at 7 p.m. Jenners, you man the BNAspace; Daisy, manage the Instagram and Twitter fan accounts.'

Jamie looked at Mel, who was smiling expectantly. 'Mel, you are head of snacks and **CHEERFULNESS**. Make sure everyone in this room has happy brains and tummies.'

Mel gave a salute, which increased room happiness by eight per cent.

The girls didn't know this yet, but this episode of *The Big Time* was going to **CHANGE THEIR LIVES FOR EVER.**

CHAPTER 7
WELCOME TO THE BIG TIME

You know when you're on a rollercoaster, and you're excited but also scared that the cars could fly off the tracks? That is how Jamie McFlair felt about tonight's episode of *The Big Time*.

The girls were packed into Jamie's little living room. Mel was **SQUIDGED** next to Jenners on the sofa, while Daisy sat on the carpet with Buttons the pug in her lap. Grandma's armchair was empty because it smelt of history.

In Jamie's eleven years of existing, she hadn't ever felt this nervous. She couldn't even sit down. She stood, toes gripped into the cream carpet with her hands on her head, staring **INTENSELY** into the television, much like Grandma would do when she was watching England in a penalty shootout.

The Big Time's opening titles burst on to the screen

as the obnoxious voiceover man shouted the rules of the competition. We'll explain them to you in a less annoying voice.

Essentially, ten acts perform every week for the judges Lady Day, Nica Konstantopolous and, of course, Barry Bigtime. If the judges decide they don't like what they see, they push a button and their chair spins away. If all three judges spin around, you're outta there. *But*, if you can hold the attention of at least one judge, you qualify for the grand final and the chance to win that cherished spot at the World Music Festival!

The host, Will Kelly, bounded on to the stage. He was short and smiley, with a face like a cartoon boy and a crop of blonde, spiky hair. Will told some below-average jokes that got above-average laughs, and welcomed *The Big Time* judges to the stage with an unnecessary amount of **RAZZMATAZZ**.

First up was Lady Day, an Australian singer who didn't even really sing any more so nobody knew why she was a judge, but she had twenty-five million Instagram followers so nobody asked questions. She wore a dress that looked like tinfoil.

The next judge was Nica Konstantopolous. Nica used to be in a band that were big before any of the girls were born. They were Jamie's mum's favourite band at university. A huge mane of curly brown hair framed her face. A dusting of gold glitter stood out on her dark skin. **SHE WAS VERY FABULOUS.**

Finally, Barry Bigtime appeared. He was wearing a purple robe made of genuine polar bear fur. His face was shiny like an action figure's, and his thin mouth

gave a sly smile below his pointed nose and slicked-back, jet-black hair. A wave of **DISGRUNTLED** bleating filled Jamie's living room as the girls expressed in unison their disgust for the disgusting man. Even Buttons the pug gave a rare growl.

The first act announced was a nervous-looking man called Malcolm who was an ice cream man. **'This guy is going to be awful,'** muttered Daisy, rolling her eyes.

'Even you couldn't pull off those tinfoil trousers,' Jenners added.

As predicted, Malcolm was not superstar material. He was quite uncoordinated and couldn't really sing.

'He has the same beard as my dad!' exclaimed Mel, which was said as a compliment, but everyone thought Mel's dad's beard was weird. Mercifully, Ice Cream Malcolm's performance came to an end after precisely forty-two seconds as all the judges spun their chairs away.

'Called it,' Jenners said.

'His vibe was all off,' agreed Daisy. They high-fived.

'He tried so hard, though, didn't he, guys?' said Mel, which was her way of saying 'this guy is hot garbage', but Mel was too nice for such brutal honesty.

Everyone knew. Even the host, Will Kelly. He returned to the stage, looked at tinfoil man and made the face you make when you hear bad news. **'Bad luck,'** said Will. 'Let's hear from the judges and see why they spun away.'

Ice Cream Malcolm looked nervous and started fiddling with his weird little beard as the judges' chairs slowly spun back around to face them. Lady Day spoke first, straightening her tinfoil dress. *Why is everyone wearing tinfoil these days?* Jamie wondered. 'Malcolm . . . Malcolm . . . darling, I think you are a great guy. You really are. Such a sweet guy and we loved having you in this competition.'

While the studio audience cheered, eyes were rolling in Jamie's living room. 'Lady Day bugs the life out of me!' said Daisy, tugging her hair in frustration.

'She needs to get on with it!' yelled Jenners.

'She's just being nice to him before saying a bad thing, like Mrs Bloggins does at school sometimes,' added Mel.

Lady Day paused and held one index finger aloft. 'But I just didn't agree with the song choice tonight.' **THE CROWD BOOED.** Jamie's eyes rolled once again. 'Plus, Malcolm darling, I'm not sure what's happening with the silver outfit thing? It just didn't really click with me, I'm afraid.'

'SHE IS LITERALLY WEARING THE SAME THING!' exclaimed Daisy. Jamie and the others had known this would annoy Daisy the most, and laughed. The next judge to speak was Nica Konstantopolous.

'Malcolm. Malcolm, my dear.' Nica was standing up. Nobody was sure why. 'You were absolutely fantastic!' The crowd whooped. Jamie's eyes were on a roll again. It was starting to make her brain dizzy.

'But she spun away!' said Jenners. **'What is this show?'**

'Nica loves everyone – it's pointless,' sighed Daisy.

'I think Nica's my favourite because she's not rude,' said Mel.

Jamie smiled at Mel. 'I think she's the one I dislike the least too.'

'Malcolm, baby,' continued Nica, **'I loved all of it.** You rocked those hot silver slacks like a champion, baby. The song happened. And it was fine. Look at these people. They love you and so do I!' The crowd were in raptures although Jamie was positive nobody really knew what on earth Nica was on about.

'A mixed bag of comments so far,' said Will Kelly, who was much shorter than Ice Cream Malcolm. He had to reach up to pull off his trademark arm-around-the-shoulder. 'But let's see what Barry has to say.'

The camera cut to Barry Bigtime. Jamie's stomach turned. He sat back in his chair with a foot on the desk, slurping on a tall glass of **CHOCOLATE MILK** through a plastic straw, grinning as if he was King Smug of Bighead Mountain.

'Malcolm, look. I'm going to be honest with you here, OK?' Barry leant forward in his chair. He took another slurp of chocolate milk. **HIS EYES NARROWED.**

'I hate you, Malcolm.' Howls of laughter erupted from the crowd. 'I hate everything about you. I hate your stupid trousers that make your legs look like burritos. I hate your silly little beard that makes you look like you have bad secrets. Do you know, Malcolm, your song was so terrible that I think my ears grew little eyes just so they could cry hysterical tears of sorrow.'

Far too many **WHOOPS** and **CACKLES** were filling the arena for a jibe that weak.

Barry was like a shark that smelt blood. 'If you, the snottiest bogey to ever find itself on the handkerchief of this show, if you somehow miraculously manage to end up on this stage again next series, Malcolm, do you know what I'm going to do? I'm going to have a trap door built into this stage that I can open up as soon as you pick up a microphone, and do you know what will be underneath that trap door waiting for you, Malcolm?'

Malcolm had absolutely no response to this, as one would imagine for a man who was being humiliated on national television.

'**Sharks,** Malcolm. A tank of hungry tiger sharks. And if we don't have budget for that? Mountain lions. Now get off the stage and think about what you've done, you absolute disgrace.'

Malcolm trudged offstage to *The Big Time*'s cheery show jingle and the last remaining cackles of the studio audience. Barry sat back, admiring his work. The girls were stunned.

'That was *so harsh*!' exclaimed Daisy 'He wasn't *that* bad?!'

'He does this every week,' grumbled Jenners, who then called Barry Bigtime a name **NOT SUITABLE** for books. 'Jamie, how is he your mum's brother? Your mum is so sound.' Jenners then stuffed some mum-provided snacks into her mouth, proving her point.

'And Barry's really . . . um . . .' began Mel, who couldn't work out the opposite to 'sound'.

'. . . an absolute *grotsack*,' finished Jamie, which was a word Grandma sometimes shouted at bad footballers.

The girls chuckled and took it in turns to shout out other rude words they'd heard Grandma say, but Jamie felt bad for Ice Cream Malcolm. Why did Uncle Barry feel the need to be so horrible to everyone? From hopeful musicians to his actual family, nobody seemed off limits. Now she was even more nervous for what was about to come.

Will Kelly returned to the screen. 'After the break, we'll find out whether **online sensation BNA** have got what it takes to make . . . *The Big Time*.'

CHAPTER 8
WELCOME BACK FROM THE AD BREAK

'And now . . .' came the cheery voice of Will Kelly, '. . . they're a big deal on the Internet, and making some waves on the underground scene, but can they make it to *The Big Time*? **Give it up for BNA!'**

Shrieks of excitement from girls and dog filled the room.

Jamie grabbed her tablet to check BNAspace. The usuals were all in the BNAspace chat, currently sharing peak excitement selfies. BrotherofBeck773 was with his entire uninterested family in his living room in Nebraska, while Scottsgal32xx was rocking out in her wheelchair along with a whole host of other **BNA SUPERFANS** from around the world in various time zones. Jamie added a selfie of all the girls and Buttons in her living room to the chat.

'Right, everyone. This is it!' said Jamie, trying to

remain as cool as possible but **SQUEALING** like Sheamus nonetheless.

Mel's head had gone. She wasn't making any sense or saying proper words.

'Come on, the boys!' yelled Jenners with such booming triumph it startled everyone in the room, as Scott, J, Beck and Harrison walked on to the stage.

'They look like actual pop stars, **this is wild!'** said Daisy, clapping enthusiastically. You knew things were going down when even Daisy couldn't keep her cool.

Jamie couldn't believe she was seeing BNA on the actual television, a programme that actual people watched. For all of the BNAniacs, this was their **BIG MOMENT.**

Lead singer J picked up the microphone.

'Hello,' he said.

The girls screamed in unison. This was easily already the performance of the night so far.

Scott began to twang the bass line as they launched into a cover of Nica Konstantopolous's 'MSN Blessenger'. **THE AUDIENCE CHEERED.**

'My heart skips a beat when you sign in,' sang J, as

Harrison and Beck launched into the familiar riff that had taken the pop world by storm twenty years ago. Nica was on her feet. The cheers in the audience turned to roars as J busted out the trademark 'MSN Blessenger' dance moves.

The crowd were loving it. The girls were loving it. Even Jamie's mum came into the living room to say how amazing it was. 'It's like being back in my uni days, Jamie! Honestly, I think I prefer their version.'

EVEN THE MUMS WERE LOVING IT.

Jamie was on her feet, dancing along. Jenners and Daisy were breaching house guest etiquette and dancing on the sofa but nobody cared. Mel looked like she was being electrocuted but it was just her special way of dancing.

Jamie was so **PROUD** of her boys. They were smashing it. She'd spent the whole year so far at school telling anyone who would listen that BNA would be the next big thing in music. Now everyone would see she was right.

As the lads went into the second chorus, there was no mistaking

77

that they were the best band to perform on *The Big Time* since the glory days of Year 3. Uncle Barry surely would have no choice but to send them to *The Big Time* final.

The camera swept through the studio and on to a close-up of Scott, who was nailing a **SICK BASS SOLO.** Jamie was awestruck . . .

Until all of a sudden, something large and soaked in a wet brown liquid sprung from nowhere and hit Scott right in the face with a big wet **PLAP.**

Jamie gasped. It seemed to wrap around Scott's head like an octopus. J looked over and was so **SHOCKED** he gave a scream, as if he'd seen a rat. Scott stumbled and crashed into Harrison. Harrison **STAGGERED** to the edge of the stage and began to teeter, legs wobbling and arms waving as if he was trying to fly himself to safety. Beck ran over to help but slipped in the brown goo, crashed into Harrison and sent the two of them off the stage and into a heap on the studio floor.

J ran to Scott and unwrapped whatever had clasped itself around his head. As he held it up in horror, it appeared to be a **PAIR OF UNDERPANTS** drenched in what was hopefully chocolate milk. The music had stopped. The camera cut to the judges as their chairs slowly spun away from the stage.

A stunned silence descended on Jamie's living room.

Jamie's stomach plunged into an icy pool of dread. Her hands **CLENCHED** into fists. As ice-cold as her insides were, her face became hot with anger and embarrassment. Her eyes darted to her friends, whose mouths hung wide open in shock. Jamie's legs gave way and she slumped into Grandma's smelly armchair, head in hands. Where had those pants come from? Deep down she knew the answer.

'**Oh, boys,** my darlings!' Lady Day said, trying to stifle her laughter. 'I feel like you've learned a lesson today.'

The only voice to be heard in Jamie's living room was the furious shouts of Jenners, who was usually the first to speak for the group when they were faced with adversity. She would always protect them from bullies and stand up for them when called for. **NOW WAS THE TIME.** Jamie dimly registered that Jenners was becoming what the girls affectionately called **JENZILLA.** This involved lots of shouting, arm movements and bad language.

'What lesson is she on about?!' snarled Daisy.

Mel was still silent. Her bottom lip stuck out and wobbled. Her big eyes filled with sadness.

'Boys, this is the music industry,' said Lady Day. 'One minute you're riding high, the next you have a soaking wet pair of dirty underpants thrown at your head. Looking at what happened on this stage today, I'm not sure you're ready to deal with the realities of the *real* music biz. I'm sorry.'

Jamie didn't think she could get any angrier, but she did. 'That has **nothing** to do with their music!'

'My boys. Let's have some real talk,' said Nica, slowly getting to her feet. Hands on hips, she shook her head and looked pensive.

'Now I've gotta say something. I've gotta say this from the bottom of my heart. Because that's my song you sang today. That song was number one in Lebanon for five straight months, OK?'

'NO ONE CARES,' yelled Jenners, eyes bulging.

'Please be nice, please be nice,' pleaded Mel, with fingers crossed on both hands.

'You guys did me proud.' There was mild applause in the studio and muttered sounds of appreciation from Jamie's living room. On-screen, Nica was nodding and had slowly raised her index finger. 'But. That craziness with the panties hitting your boy right in his face? Stumbling around like a zombie? Sliding around the stage like he was the lead in *Pantsface On Ice*! That was some of the funniest stuff I've seen in thirty years of the music business. Nobody's going to forget that. Y'all may as well change your names to The Underpanties Boys.' Nica broke down into laughter.

The camera cut to Scott's embarrassed, sodden face. J's expression of horror hadn't changed since the underpants had invaded their performance. Harrison and Beck had just managed to clamber back on to the stage. If the ordeal hadn't been enough, Barry Bigtime's sneering face flashed up on-screen. Jamie was so angry she was looking for things to throw at the television. Could she frisbee her mum's decorative bowl of potpourri into the screen? No. **DESTRUCTIVE RAGE WASN'T HER STYLE.** It's not like they could ever afford to replace anything she broke. She leant forward, seething silently, staring into Barry Bigtime's beady eyes.

Barry's eyebrow was raised. His wry smile signalled that he was about to speak.

'Look, boys. I'm going to be honest with you. There's one thing I can't stand – **arrogance.** It felt like you thought you were too *big* for *The Big Time* and then what we saw was a boring performance. You YouTube bands need to know that you aren't as good as you think you are. So I removed my underpants, swilled them around in my chocolate milk and threw them at your stupid head. **Yes, you.**' He pointed at Scott.

If Jamie's brain were a volcano, magma would be pouring out of her eyes, ears and nose. She could hardly breathe. 'You four morons should be thanking me for this lesson because you needed a serious wake-up call. It's just a shame it had to be taught to you in front of the entire world. Now get off my stage before I think about how good you'd look in a shark tank.' Barry **GRINNED** as the audience howled with laughter.

Jamie reached towards the coffee table, picked up two handfuls of potpourri from the bowl and squashed them into crumbs. She couldn't face her friends, let alone the BNAspace group chat. She stared at Uncle Barry Bigtime. The man who'd stolen her grandma's house, stolen her mum's money. The man responsible for Jamie having to share a room with old ladies, pigs and bottom ghosts. And now he had even **HUMILIATED** BNA in front of the world. He was not going to get away with this any more. In that moment Jamie decided Barry was going to get what he deserved. **THIS WAS THE FINAL STRAW.**

CHAPTER 9
That's Show Business

'CLEAR!' came the shout from the floor manager, signalling to everyone that *The Big Time* was off-air. Barry strutted down the side of the arena as huge studio cameras on cranes swung overhead. Hundreds of crew members scattered across the studio floor, shouting things like **'I'M SO STRESSED'** and **'I HAVEN'T SLEPT IN WEEKS'.** They were working in TV, though, so even if they were sad, everyone else thought they were cool.

As Barry got closer to the double doors which read **BACKSTAGE ONLY**, a cameraman leapt in front of him wearing a black T-shirt that read 'Montage'. This cameraman's job was to make cool slow-motion montages for the show. He was the best of the best and had made montages for the biggest moments in history: the Olympic opening ceremonies, World Cup finals and television baking competitions. Barry strolled past and gave the camera **A WINK,** which was weird enough in normal motion but would be exactly 240 times weirder in slow motion. He burst through the backstage doors, and disappeared down the corridor.

Barry Bigtime sat in his dressing room doing his favourite thing: looking at his own face in the mirror. The mirror, like all good showbiz mirrors, was surrounded by light bulbs, but even these light bulbs were decorated with Barry Bigtime's grinning face. In front of the mirror was a shelf filled with a huge number of bottles, potions and tools used to make Barry look **FAR BETTER** than he did in real life.

That was a close call, thought Barry. *Why didn't any of the morons in my team tell me that this BNA bunch were actually good?!*

He briefly considered a world in which raw talent alone could have made a band like BNA a success. He shuddered.

There was a knock at the door. **'Enter,'** said Barry as if he was a guardian to an ancient treasure trove.

In bumbled Winston (who looked even more

stressed than when we last saw him, in a pair of tiny trunks riding a dolphin).

'You,' Barry said, and slammed his fist into the shelf of bottles and ointments, scattering them everywhere.

Here's a fun game: pay close attention to this next bit and see if you can pinpoint the moment where Barry's rage goes from bubbling pasta pan to full-blown shaken-cola-bottle **EXPLOSION.**

'What on EARTH happened out there tonight, Winston?! Are you an imbecile, or are you trying to put us all out of business?'

'I . . . I . . . I have . . .' stammered Winston.

'*Oooh, I have*,' squealed Barry in a mock baby voice. 'How were this BNA bunch allowed to be on the show?!'

'I . . . I think you insisted . . .' stammered Winston. But unfortunately for poor Winston, facts were not helpful at this point.

SPOILER ALERT – THE SHAKEN-COLA-BOTTLE MOMENT IS NOW.

'I'm not sure if you remember, but I am on the brink of losing **EVERYTHING!** I NEED TO MAKE THE NEXT BIG

86

BOYBAND. And we're here giving these BNA Internet darlings TELEVISION EXPOSURE?!' Barry raised both his arms and, like a purple tidal wave, swept all the remaining bottles, beakers and glassware from the shelf. **BARRY LOVED HIS THEATRICS.**

'I was only doin' what was asked!' pleaded Winston, cowering against the dressing room door, shaking like a dog doing a **POO.** 'You told me to do whatever it took to get them on the show! I didn't think they'd be *that* good!'

'GOOD?' yelled Barry, leaping to his feet. He picked up a bottle of incisor shiner and threw it at Winston's head, where it luckily missed by inches and smashed into the wall. **'THEY WERE FANTASTIC!** They were one of the best raw talents I've ever heard. They would take the world by storm! If we let raw talent run wild we'll be out of business! That's why *The Big Time* is fixed so only MY boybands can ever win! Winston, you are lucky I acted when I did because if I hadn't thrown those chocolate-milkshake-sodden underpants at their stupid, lovely, talented heads, EVERYONE would be buying THEIR music! People would think they could succeed in this industry without MY help. I need BNA GONE and GONE FOR GOOD.'

'But, Barry, I think their careers are pretty much done, y'know.'

'It's not enough. We can't risk it. Winston. I want. Them. Gone. Not just gone. **Gone gone.**'

'I . . .' spluttered Winston.

'I could lose EVERYTHING and you have nothing to say?' Barry scowled. 'You're fired! Now get out of here before you're fed to the sharks!' Fearing for his life and with no chance to protest, Winston hurried from the room, more bottles flying after him.

Barry slumped into his chair. It was **EXHAUSTING** dealing with morons. Next to the showbiz mirror was an intercom that connected to Barry's assistant, Vanessa. He pressed the button.

'Vanessa, I've fired Winston. Please make sure he leaves.' Barry paused to think. 'I'm also firing Hector Macaulay and Marcos Paul. Please let them know.'

'I will,' said Vanessa, who was used to this.

'And could you send Johnny Whopper in here. Right now. **Like almost instantly,** please. I want to look up from this intercom and immediately see his stupid little—'

'You wanted to see me, sir?' Johnny's head appeared from behind the door. His skeletal frame **SLITHERED** in behind him. Johnny had a mop of oily hair and was wearing a sharp, dark purple suit. He was the head of Barry's truth-twisting team. It was his job to deceive people into thinking that bad boybands were actually good boybands or that nasty people were actually nice people and that bad ideas were actually great ideas. His **LIES** had made Barry very rich and had got The Fenton Dogz lots of undeserved radio airtime.

'What a mess this all is, Johnny,' sighed Barry.

'I can get housekeeping in to clear this up right away, sir. No problem,' said Johnny, reaching for his phone.

'Not this mess, you fool. I don't care about that.' He picked up a bottle from the floor that contained eyebrow shampoo and squeezed the contents all over the floor. 'The mess that happened out there.'

'Oh yes, sir. Terrible mess. BNA, awful band.' Johnny nodded.

'Well, no, they were **really good,** that's the mess,' corrected Barry.

'Oh yes, sir. Tremendous band. Excellent.' Johnny nodded like one of those little plastic dogs people sometimes have in their cars.

'I need them out of the way before we create the next big boyband.' Barry stroked his shiny chin. 'Johnny, I want that clip of those underpants hitting that boy – Clott, Scott, whatever his name is – I want the exact moment pants meet with face all over the Internet. Get on to the **MEME TEAM** and have them working through the night. I don't want anyone talking about anything BNA-related that doesn't involve chocolate underpants. I want every YouTuber reacting to the moment those pants hit that boy in the face. I want #BNAisoverparty and #BNAcancelled trending on every page in the solar system. If anyone online tries to talk about how good BNA's music is, send out the **TROLLS.** Do you know what will happen to you if all this doesn't happen, Johnny?'

Johnny had a fair idea that it would probably involve sharks. He nodded sagely.

'Exactly,' said Barry. 'Now get on it.'

Johnny slunk out of the dressing room. Barry went back to his chair and admired the surrounding wreckage and then his own face once again. He knew there was one more big problem. *I need to make a boyband and fast, but I still don't have any ingredients. All I have is my fantastically successful boybands of the past that people apparently don't want to see again.*

Fizz . . . BANG.

One of the lightbulbs around his showbiz mirror blew out. It was a real evil genius moment because it happened exactly as Barry had an idea. **AN IDEA THAT COULD SAVE HIM . . .**

CHAPTER 10
THE CHOCOLATE UNDERPANTS BOYS

Welcome to Crudwell Junior School! Which, according to their website, is a place where children are encouraged to be the **VERY BEST THEY CAN BE!** It has an outstanding Ofsted report and a commitment to growing a culture of creativity without limits! Jamie, Daisy, Jenners and Mel saw that someone had certainly exercised the culture of **CREATIVITY** as they climbed up to the school treehouse.

BNA EAT UNDERPANTS FOR BREAKFAST

was scribbled in crayon on the treehouse wall. Jamie sighed. BNA had become a laughing stock and their social media numbers had **PLUMMETED** overnight.

Jamie and the others had retreated here to escape the jeers and taunts of the school. But because everyone knew how much Jamie loved BNA, it turned out there was no escape. It had been a **TOUGH** day.

Even Grandma had teased Jamie while taking her medicine. Dominic had made a boring joke about them over breakfast. Jamie had to turn her phone off as she was being inundated with BNA underpants memes. There was Harrison falling off the stage accompanied by a **'FALLING INTO MONDAY LIKE . . .'** caption, and the still image of the underpants hitting Scott's face with the caption, 'When you think you aced the test then get the results back.'

Jamie wondered who made all of these memes so quickly.

Their day didn't get any better. Even Daisy, one of the coolest girls in the school, was being teased. 'Only a stupid BNA fan would wear a silly beret like that,' shouted Filbert Bennigan across the English classroom. Daisy touched a hand to her beret and **GASPED.** The real joke was on Filbert Bennigan though because his name was Filbert Bennigan.

Then, as Mel was leaving her classroom for break time, a pale, skinny figure with a pair of PE shorts

wrapped around his
head blundered in her direction with his
arms outstretched. 'OH NO, I'M SCOTT
FROM BNA, **SOMEONE HELP,'** wailed
Benji Leighton to the cackles of the other Year 6s. Mel
was so startled, a loud panic fart escaped from her
bottom to howls of laughter. Then, at break time,
Tobias Merryweather tried to launch a pants attack at
the girls.

It's worth us pausing for a second here to tell you
about Tobias Merryweather, which is a shame because
he is not a nice character in this book and doesn't
deserve the airtime. His only redeeming feature was
his **FABULOUS** golden curls, which wouldn't look out
of place in a shampoo advert. He had bright blue eyes
and a mole the size of a rice crispie on the side of his
nose. Tobias came from a family that was so
PRETENTIOUS even his dog sounded posh when it
barked. His dad owned a company that bought
numbers off the Internet and then sold them to people
who couldn't really afford them. His mum used to be
an artist but then invented a skin cream out of an

avocado and now sells it to her friends who own boats. His parents were too busy and too rich to pay him any attention, so he **CRAVED** it from his classmates.

Just as Jamie, Jenners, Daisy and Mel were reunited at break time, Tobias jumped out of a bush. **'BNA ARE CANCELLED,'** he shouted, drawing his arm back to hurl a pair of pants at Jamie's head.

But Jenners's deceiving pace caught Tobias by surprise. She grabbed his arm mid-throw, picked Tobias up over her head and threatened to chuck him into the conservation pond unless he withdrew his unflattering BNA opinions.

UNFORTUNATELY, with Tobias held aloft, Jenners was busted by Miss Leigh-Johnson, who banned her from football practice for a week. It was not ideal for Jenners's football career but would be good additional bonus time to plan revenge on Barry Bigtime. The girls had then retreated to the treehouse to form their plan.

'Why don't we bust into Barry's garden, **do a poo on the lawns,** then knock on his door and run away?' yelled Jenners, who was on the brink of Jenzilla.

'I'm not pooing on anyone's grass, Jenners, **that's gross,'** said Daisy firmly.

'Me neither,' said Mel. 'What if I get there and I can't go?' Thinking about it was giving her anxiety.

Jamie didn't feel like it was punishment enough.

'We wouldn't be able to get past the gates. He has electronic security thingies to stop people getting in,'

she said. 'Grandma gets to visit
him once a year on her birthday and even
she has to go through security gates.'

'Oh please, I could hack his stupid gates,' scoffed
Jenners. Jenners was notorious for her computing
skills. Not only had she inherited her mum's physical
prowess but also her dad's **INTELLIGENCE.** 'Remember,
in the summer holidays? Catherine Boden lost her
bear, Mr Bearface, in Crudwell shopping centre, so I
hacked into the CCTV systems to see if I could
track him down. I managed to spot him outside
Milano's Pizza.'

It was true. Jenners was a school hero that day.
Today, Catherine Boden had called them all BN-lame-
ohs in Maths. People had such short memories.

'Why don't we spread some sort of vicious rumour
online?' suggested Daisy. 'We could make a vicious
Barry Bigtime meme to make him seem super lame?'

'Uncle Barry has loads of haters, though,' said
Jamie. 'He loves it, it's like he gets more **powerful**
the angrier people get at what he says.'

'What I don't understand,' said Daisy, 'is why Barry

Bigtime didn't just send them through? BNA were clearly loads better than any band that have been on *The Big Time* since we've been in junior school. **Why did he throw the pants?'**

Jamie frowned. It had been bothering her too.

'And Beck said in their YouTube video that they were "begging" for the boys to appear on the show, so why waste perfectly good chocolate milk by throwing pants at them?' Daisy added.

'Maybe he had a good reason?' suggested Mel, who liked to try to see the good in everyone.

'A reason . . .' mused Jamie. She looked up with a start. 'Jenners, do you think you could **hack into the CCTV** of *The Big Time*'s television studios?' asked Jamie.

Jenners raised an eyebrow. 'Depends on the strength of their firewall. Why?'

'I want to know what happened backstage at the show. Like Mel said, there **must** be a reason for what Barry did that we aren't seeing.'

'Also, we might spot him doing something embarrassing backstage which may make for some

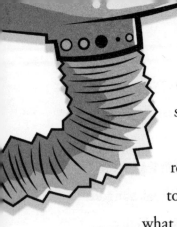

dank memes,' added Daisy. 'Just saying.'

You know when someone has a really good idea and everyone starts to bubble with excitement? That's what was happening in the treehouse.

'We could head to the computer room at lunchtime!' said Jenners, jumping to her feet but **BASHING** her head on the roof.

'Isn't hacking into security systems against Mr Javanerd's IT rules?' asked Mel, chewing on a fingernail. Mr Javanerd was the school IT technician. He was **VERY STRICT** and a Level 92 *GoblinQuest* Paladin so he was not someone to mess with.

'Are the school computers going to be fast enough?' asked Daisy. 'It takes me at least nine seconds to load Instagram.'

The girls looked to Jamie as they knew she was the best at making plans. **SHE SMILED.**

'Jenners, you sneak out of class five minutes early to secure a good computer that isn't slow. Daisy, you're the smoothest talker – you distract Mr Javanerd. Mel and I will keep watch for anyone else who tries to poke their nose in, like Tobias Merryweather and his cronies.'

The girls nodded and started to climb out of the treehouse as the bell for the end of break rang out.

'Who still says **"cronies"**?' asked Daisy.

CHAPTER 11
BARRYMANIA

Barry skipped down one of the nonsensically decorated hallways in his mansion, singing **'I'VE GOT A HEINOUS EVIL PLAN'** to the tune of 'Yankee Doodle Dandy'. He reached the Brilliant Hall, which was like a Great Hall but even better. It was a room which had hosted many a nice time, enjoyed by many a terrible person.

He whipped out his phone from his lilac pantaloons and composed an email with unnecessarily pompous finger jabs.

All staff report to the Brilliant Hall immediately. Urgent. Bring snacks and chocolate milk.

Now, some of the staff at Barry Bigtime's mansion weren't the usual types you would find tending to the upkeep of a suburban estate. In fact, they weren't the types you would find **ANYWHERE** in the world. Prepare yourselves, please, because some of the staff at Barry Bigtime's mansion weren't exactly humans at all, but some of Barry's early experiments . . .

The first to arrive was **SLOTTAPUSS.** Barry had found Slottapuss the rat snuffling in some garbage behind his mansion many years ago. Back then, Slottapuss had been a normal rodent going about his usual disgusting duties. Now he was six feet tall, had the muscular arms and legs of a human man and could play Grade 6 piano. He was wearing a pair of designer shades balanced on his long, brown, hairy snout, a grubby leather jacket on top of a dirty greying vest and frayed blue jeans.

He was Barry's **CHIEF HENCHMAN.** Whenever a curious journalist managed to intrude on the Bigtime mansion grounds, Slottapuss would slink through the mansion sewers and haul himself out of a drain in the garden. The last thing the undesirable would see was their own twisted, terrified face staring back at them in the reflection of Slottapuss's sunglasses.

The distant clicking of pincers indicated that

FLOBSTER was about to arrive. Flobster was half-man, half-lobster. His lobster head hung over a large, doughy belly that was covered with a dirty apron. His black eyes were shining, his antennae twitching and, as ever, those pincers were a-clicking. He was also a fine jazz musician.

Behind Flobster lumbered **HENRIK,** a seven-foot grizzly bear with two large human ears. He wore a waistcoat and a fez and occasionally would twiddle a mandolin.

Finally, a team of humans arrived. They were arguably worse than all of the beasts put together. These human creatures were Barry Bigtime's truth-twisting team. You remember **JOHNNY WHOPPER** from earlier? The man in charge of all the lies? Well, he was there, along with **TRIXIE** and **AMELIA.** They were as slippery as Flobster and as cunning as Slottapuss.

Then followed **FABIO** the chef, **AUGUSTUS** the gardener and a few other less terrible but ultimately unimportant characters, so let's skip past them.

The congregation gathered on the Brilliant Hall dance floor as Barry took to the stage. He clapped

three times to get everyone's attention, forgetting that this would activate his giant disco ball to descend from the ceiling and begin blaring track one from the album *Whiffy Cheese Pop Hits*.

He glared at Flobster, who clumsily and slowly clambered over everyone to halt the **HULLABALOO** and resume dramatic silence.

'Trusted friends and mutant minions,' bellowed Barry. 'We have the gravest situation on our hands—'

'Are the inland revenue troubling us again, boss?' yelped Henrik.

Barry closed his eyes. 'If you interrupt me again, I'll make sure **deep-fried bear thighs** are the hottest food trend this year.'

Henrik gulped. Barry had made the same threat to Jimmy the penguin last autumn, and Jimmy had become the main course at the staff Christmas party.

'We have a situation. Our stores of boyband ingredients have run dry. We are devoid of dimples, smiles, skinny jeans, hairstyles, cheese, everything.'

There was a **GASP.**

'We have also, due to some trifling legal matters, some unfortunate investments and the public being too stupid to recognise talent when they hear it, been left in quite some financial difficulty. If we don't quickly produce the finest boyband the world has ever seen, then BigTime Manor, BigTime Productions, *The Big Time* and BigTimeNiceTimes Inc. will be no more.'

There was another, **LOUDER GASP.**

'Remember, if I go down, I'm taking each and every one of you with me. But if we succeed, we would be so rich we could replace the water in the swimming pools with cold hard cash and, most importantly, we could build the rollercoaster that *all* of us yearn for.'

Truthfully, nobody other than Barry gave one toot about a garden rollercoaster, but nobody had the courage to have personal dreams of their own.

'So, I have come up with a solution.'

There were looks of terror in the room.

'We have made some great boybands in the past. Why make more when we can **recycle** what we don't need any more?'

Johnny Whopper stepped forward, nervously running his skeletal fingers through his oily mop of black hair. 'Sir, if you don't mind me saying, bravo.' He clapped his hands as if he had heard the solution to all the conflicts in the world. 'You mean to use the boyband generator to take all of the best parts and talents of our previous boybands, and extract them to make the best boyband in the world?'

'That is **precisely what we're doing,** my grubby little friend. The *best* boybands I have ever produced will be here, in this mansion, this Friday night for a party. We'll work all through Saturday and our new band will debut on *The Big Time* that evening, then they'll qualify for the final, which incidentally they will win with a little help from my friends. *Then* they will go on to steal the show at the **World Music Festival,** AND WE – well, more like **I – WILL BE RICH!'** Barry hissed while wringing his hands together. Being on the stage had made Barry act like a cliché of an evil genius.

'We should invite the underpants boyband! They were pretty good, I thought!' blurted Henrik.

SILENCE.

Slottapuss edged his sunglasses down his long, thin nose in disbelief. Even for Henrik, this was a **DUMB** thing to say. The whole staff were very aware how sensitive Barry had been to the whole BNA debacle.

'What did you just say?' said Barry, his voice dangerously soft.

'I don't . . . I don't think I said anything actually . . . Maybe it was Slottapuss? We sometimes sound similar.'

Barry hopped down from the stage and began to walk slowly towards Henrik.

'I am having a party with *my* boybands aka *proper* boybands, **the best** in the world. Why would I invite those snivelling, pant-sniffing, gelatinous tapeworms to a BigTime-sponsored evening of organised fun?

'I . . . I . . .' stammered Henrik, raising his paws as if he was expecting Barry to pounce on him at any moment. He was trembling so much his fez almost wobbled off the top of his head.

'*I . . . I . . .*' mimicked Barry in his baby voice, striding towards Henrik with more purpose. 'You, Henrik are the biggest, most complete, total, ten-out-of-ten, record-breaking—'

Barry froze mid-sentence. The biggest, most **EVIL** lightbulb in his brain had just flicked on.

'. . . **genius** who ever lived,' he finished softly, a grin breaking out on his shiny face.

Henrik felt like the most confused bear who'd ever lived, and this was a bear who spent a lot of his time being confused.

'Truth-twisters, you are to contact every boyband we have ever produced. You are to tell them that we are going to throw the biggest party the world has ever seen.'

'Is it going to be bigger than Billy Clarkson's sixtieth?!' shrieked Amelia. Billy Clarkson's sixtieth had got so out of hand that some of the guests had ended up in space.

'No, fool,' snapped Barry. **'It's a lie.** You just need to say whatever you need to say to ensure *all* of these boys arrive at the mansion. Do I have to tell you how to do your job?'

Amelia, red-faced, lowered her gaze to the ground.

'Say whatever it takes to get the bands here, plus I want you to invite four very special guests.'

'Who?' asked Amelia.

'BNA,' said Barry. 'They might not be the best band in the world . . . but they are certainly going to be part of one.'

'But . . . sir . . . are they going to want to come to your party after you turned them into a global laughing stock?' asked Trixie.

Barry closed his eyes once more, balled his hands into fists and gritted his teeth. 'You will find a way to get BNA to this party. If you don't, then you can explain yourselves to the **sharks.'**

CHAPTER 12
HACKING THE SYSTEM

Jenners had a **GUARANTEED** way to get out of class five minutes before lunch. Jamie, Daisy and Mel watched her slowly walk up to their Year 6 teacher, Mr Durdy, a large, boring man with thin, balding hair. Jenners made herself look as scared as possible.

'Mr Durdy, I have an upset tummy and I really need to visit the bathroom. If I don't go, sometimes there's nothing I can do before it's too late and my mother said she doesn't ever want to witness what she saw that day ever again . . .'

Mr Durdy's bulbous eyes widened as he imagined the atrocities that could occur.

'Oh goodness, quick, go, go, go, now, out, **immediately,'** he said, flapping his arms at Jenners. She bolted out of the room.

The class had just finished an art lesson and Daisy

had made a diagram of the Internet using pasta pieces to show Mr Javanerd as part of their **DISTRACTION** plan. Mr Durdy gave the word for the class to pack away their things and Jamie, Mel and Daisy's table was like a whirlwind as pasta, glue, pens and paper disappeared in record time. They stood by their chairs looking as ready to be sent out to lunch as they could possibly be. Hands by sides, straight-backed, fingers on lips.

To Jamie's annoyance, Tobias Merryweather's table was still a **SHAMBLES** and he wasn't even helping to tidy. Felt pens, colouring pencils and papers were strewn everywhere. Tobias was rocking on his chair (which you weren't allowed to do) while juggling Pritt Sticks to the applause of Gaby Nicklin, Filbert Bennigan, Benji Leighton and Wilbur Lyons, whose jowls wobbled when he laughed.

'It looks like we're waiting for Tobias's table,' droned Mr Durdy. 'What a shame, Tobias, Gaby, Wilbur, Benji and Filbert, that you're holding **everybody** up from having their lunch today.'

Often at school, getting a teacher is like rolling a dice, but having to stick with that number for a whole year. In Year 5 the girls had rolled a solid six with Mrs Bloggins. She used to treat the girls like grown-ups and was generally **INSPIRATIONAL AND FABULOUS.** But this year they had rolled a one, and were destined to plod through the school year, one square at a time, as a dull, scruffy man droned at them like a robot.

Tobias looked completely **UNBOTHERED** by Mr Durdy's scorn. 'I'm **SO** sorry, Mr Durdy.' Tobias rolled his big blue eyes, picked up one felt-tip pen from the many that were still scattered across the table and walked to the pen pot, taking large, slow comedy steps, golden curls bouncing everywhere. The class were already two minutes late for lunch now and, more importantly, Jamie, Daisy and Mel were two minutes late to help Jenners.

Jamie, never one to stand by and watch a plan be jeopardised, walked over to the table, eyes as **fiery as her hair,** and scooped up the felt pens.

'Someone's keen for lunch,' Tobias sneered. 'What's on the menu, Lame-y? Boiled underpants with your favourite chocolate milk gravy?'

The other boys on the table laughed way louder

than that mediocre joke deserved.

Everything Tobias said was filled with so much pomposity, his curly head bobbed around with every word.

Maybe I could jam the felt pens up his nose, thought Jamie. Tobias's nose was quite large, with prominent nostrils that would easily accommodate a pen.

We won't be any help to Jenners if we have to miss our lunchtime! pleaded Jamie's conscience.

'Jamie McFlair, why are you not at your table?' droned Mr Durdy.

'She's taking our felt-tip pens!' shouted Benji.

'I'm helping!' yelled Jamie.

'Excuse me,' said Mr Durdy in that annoying way teachers begin a telling-off. 'That's not how we speak to teachers at Crudwell Junior School, is it, Jamie McFlair? Your table can leave for lunch last.'

The injustice! Jamie could have screamed as she watched Tobias and his friends skip out of the door to lunch. **'But Mr Durdy . . .'** Jamie began, but Daisy put a hand on her shoulder.

'Just leave it,' she whispered.

Daisy was right. Time was precious and it was ticking. If she argued and this lunchtime was taken away from them, the girls' only other option would be to use the Crudwell Library, whose computers were **SO SLOW,** it was an insult to the Internet. Besides, *The Big Time* security footage could be archived and gone tomorrow. She kept **SCHTUM.**

Jamie, Daisy and Mel stood super straight by their table in the now empty classroom. Mr Durdy slowly walked to his desk, shuffled some papers, looked at his watch, sipped from his cold tea, scratched his balding head, straightened his ugly mustard tie, looked out of the window, scratched the dimple on his chin and **FINALLY** let Jamie, Mel and Daisy leave for lunch.

But in the cloakroom, Tobias Merryweather was waiting for them, flanked by Benji Leighton, Wilbur Lyons and Filbert Bennigan. Just so you know, these three boys also had parents who owned their own boats. Tobias was tossing an apple up and down in his hand. Wilbur tried to do the same but dropped his.

'Maybe you should just be a fan of

our band now, **Lame-y McHair,**' said Tobias.

Jamie did a big fake laugh. The boys had made a few YouTube videos covering Baezone songs, which about six people had watched. 'Oh? Did you get good suddenly?'

Tobias scowled. 'You do realise we are going to be super famous, **Stainy McUnderWEAR!**'

'We're loads better than BN-lame,' added Benji, eyeballing Jamie through his thick-rimmed glasses and from behind some rogue strands of floppy black hair.

'**Mmm,** I don't know, I think I'd rather watch my grandma eat porridge for ever than listen to one of your songs,' Jamie said. Mel giggled and Daisy gave the boys a **CHALLENGING** eyebrow.

'We've actually been invited to a super-exclusive party to be signed to a record label, and we're going to be turned into superstars!' yelled Wilbur Lyons, whose jowls waggled as he got cross, which was often. His quiff defied gravity.

Jamie, still annoyed about the art class injustice and mad at having her time wasted, snapped. '**You're a liar!**' she yelled.

'Yeah, liar liar pants on fire,' squealed Mel.

At the sound of raised voices, a few Year 6s gathered round to watch.

'More like pants covered in chocolate. Am I right, guys?' sneered Tobias to a gaggle of chuckles.

(Because Tobias was popular, people would laugh at things he said even when they were definitely not funny. **YOU KNOW THE SORT.**)

Tobias ripped the sticker off his lunch apple and ate it slowly in front of them, staring the girls straight in the eyes as he did. Two of the other boys did the same, even though Wilbur's had been on the floor. Benji, the final member of the squad, didn't have an apple, so started slowly peeling his orange, trying hard not to be annoyed as he sprayed sticky citrus juice all over himself.

Jamie had **TOLERATED** these boys for fifteen and a half terms now, but it was important to stay calm because they desperately needed to get to Jenners. She was about to walk away but there was a **FLASH** of white and a pair of underpants were sitting on Mel's head.

'I'll show you where you can put those pants!' shouted Jamie. Before her brain could stop her, Jamie had swiped the pants from Mel's head and made a leap for Tobias Merryweather, trying to pull them over his **VOLUMINOUS** curls.

The two of them were grappling and bashing into PE bags and coats when a voice yelled, **'WHAT ON EARTH IS GOING ON HERE?'**

Mrs Bloggins had arrived.

CHAPTER 13
THE CYBER LAB SHOWDOWN

Mrs Bloggins wasn't like any teacher at Crudwell Junior School. She wasn't like any teacher you've ever seen before. She was wearing a massive furry blue coat and a long leopard-print dress. She **SAUNTERED** into the cloakroom on bright red high heels, eyes fixed on the children.

Jamie felt **ASHAMED** that her favourite teacher had seen her acting so badly and mad at Tobias all over again for starting it.

Tobias Merryweather yelled mumbled pleas for help, with one eye either side of the gusset of the underpants.

'Jamie McFlair, Melissa Grainger, Daisy Palmer: my classroom, please. Don't worry, Mr Durdy, **I'll deal with this,'** she said as the Year 6 teacher stood **DUMBFOUNDED** at the commotion outside his classroom.

Mrs Bloggins took them into their old Year 5 classroom and pointed to three chairs by her desk.

'Sit, please, girls.'

'Can we not sit on the beanbags?' asked Daisy, still clutching her pasta picture of the Internet.

'Nope. You're in trouble and besides, I couldn't get down there today. **Not in this dress.'**

This was disastrous – they were running out of valuable time to help Jenners. The girls obeyed, looking embarrassed, as Mrs Bloggins sat down behind her desk, which was covered in books and papers. She gave each girl a crystal glass and poured three hearty servings of Ribena.

'Do you mind if I eat?' Mrs Bloggins asked, but

before they could answer she'd produced a big bag of kale from nowhere, torn it open and begun **CHOMPING** down on the leaves like a hungry giraffe.

'What on earth has got into you, Jamie?' asked Mrs Bloggins. 'Fighting in the cloakroom? That's not the Jamie McFlair I remember.'

The girls explained what had happened on *The Big Time* over the weekend.

'We've been teased all day about BNA, and I just got really cross for a second,' said Jamie, looking down at the floor.

'I know Tobias Merryweather is a **constant source of vexation,**' said Mrs Bloggins. 'But when anything unfortunate happens to him, it means I have to converse with his mother, which is not how I like spending my time. Try to avoid manhandling him if you can.'

'But the whole school is laughing at us,' said Daisy.

Mrs Bloggins swallowed the last of her kale leaves and washed them down with a glass of her own special Ribena.

'I can tell you a good story about feeling like you're

a laughing stock to the world,' began Mrs Bloggins.

Uh-oh, Jamie thought, *this sounds like a useful-but-long life lesson.* The girls loved Mrs Bloggins's **WISDOM**. It was thorough and lengthy and often featured her ex-husband, which was great when they were supposed to be doing maths, but not so great when they were already ten minutes late to meet Jenners, who would undoubtedly be having her own personal rage.

'Mrs Bloggins . . .' began Daisy, eyes wide and full of fear. 'I think I have an upset tummy and I really need to visit the bathroom.'

Mrs Bloggins rolled her eyes.

'Don't try that on me, Daisy. OK, I'll let you girls go. Just promise me you'll **stay away** from Tobias Merryweather? That boy **thrives off attention** and I won't stand for three clever girls letting themselves down. Understood?'

The girls nodded, thanked Mrs Bloggins and **DARTED** out of the room.

The IT room was on the other side of the school, across the playground. They ran as fast as they could, narrowly missing Tommy Gerkins, who was chasing his friends pretending to be a giant **EVIL SUNFLOWER,** and ducking under the arms of Jimmy Milton, who was playing stuck in the mud, thus accidentally freeing him.

'Hey, Milton, you're not free! Those girls aren't playing!' came a yell. It was too late. Jimmy Milton was screaming the word **'FREEDOM!'** like he'd just escaped from prison.

They burst through the doors of the Year 4 cloakroom, sliding to the left, down the corridor to the IT room, which the headmistress had called the **'CYBER LAB'** to make it sound cool.

They burst in and spotted Jenners on a computer in the corner.

'Where on earth have you been?' said Jenners in much ruder words than written in this book.

Jamie explained the felt pens, the underpants, Tobias Merryweather and Mrs Bloggins.

'Can someone deal with Mr Javanerd? He keeps snooping!' grumbled Jenners.

Mr Javanerd was super protective of the computers. He thought every website could give the network a virus and would not take kindly to students **HACKING** into the security systems of a television studio.

Daisy, with her pasta picture still in her hands, knocked on the IT office door and in her sweetest voice said, 'Oh, Mr Javanerd, you must see this picture I've made for you of the Internet! I was hoping you could help me label some of the trickier parts.'

Daisy went into the office and closed the door.

'I got bored waiting for you three, so I risked it and I've already started,' Jenners said with a **SMUG** smile.

'Have you actually?' Jamie said, impressed with her friend's audacity. 'How is it going?'

'So far so good. I got past their firewall *so* easily.'

'How did you do that so fast?'

You know the phrase 'all brawn, no brains'? Well, that certainly didn't apply to Jenners. When she inevitably becomes a professional footballer in a few years, she'll be the best and **SMARTEST** on the pitch.

'I hacked into my mum's Facebook and messaged her mate Dillis, who works at the TV studio on Saturday nights, pretending to be my mum, asking her who works in the CCTV department. Dillis told me it was some fella called Percy, who according to his Twitter is **obsessed** with baby monkeys. So I sent him a link to a video of a baby monkey riding a pig, but *actually* it was a trojan horse virus that will allow me access to the whole of the TV studio's server.'

Jamie and Mel's mouths **DROPPED OPEN.**

'But these stupid school computers are so slow, it's taking ages to actually download the CCTV videos.'

'We don't have much time,' said Mel. 'I think I can hear the Year 4s going in for their lunch – our sitting will be soon . . .'

'Watchya girls doing?' said a nasally voice. Jamie turned to see Benji Leighton slink into the lab.

'Go away, Benji,' sighed Jamie. She didn't want to see him or any of Tobias's other friends again so soon. Benji was one of the **WORST**: if he wasn't following Tobias around laughing at his jokes while not understanding them, he'd be in the computer room playing *Farm Village*.

He also spat when he talked, which isn't an essential detail to the story but was still **EXTRA ANNOYING.**

'I hope you ladies aren't using the school computers for funny business. If you give them viruses then Mr Javanerd will get cross.'

'Please can you leave us alone?' said Mel nicely.

'Benji, if you don't buzz off I will **throw you out of the window,'** said Jenners.

'You're not allowed to threaten violence!' squealed Benji. 'I'm going to tell Mr Javanerd.'

'Please, Benji, don't tell on us,' **BEGGED** Jamie.

'I'm in!' shouted Jenners. 'Which CCTV camera should I look at? Look! I can see the boys in the corridor before their song . . . Oh they look nervous . . . Guys, Scott's doing the "Four Nights" dance! That's so funny, they should do a video of just that.'

It was important not to get distracted, though every fibre of Jamie's being wanted to watch more of Scott's 'Four Nights' dance. 'Where's Uncle Barry? Can you spot him in any of the backstage areas?'

'Are you playing hacking?' gasped Benji. In the excitement, they'd briefly overlooked his existence. 'Oh my dilly gon garny, that is against *all* the rules of the computer room! **I'm going to tell!**'

'Benji! Honestly, don't tell, this is really important!' said Jamie, her words rushed with urgency, but she could see Benji wasn't to be reasoned with after she'd just attacked his leader with underwear.

'We'll do anything, honestly,' pleaded Mel.

'Anything?' asked Benji in a way that made all of the girls' toes curl.

'Anything,' said Jamie, gritting her teeth.

'Then I want to go to the Hallow'een disco with Jennifer,' said Benji, **BLUSHING.** Jennifer was what the rest of the school called Jenners because that was her name.

Jenners will not be keen for this, thought Jamie, fearing combustion.

'Absolutely not. Gross. No way,' said Jenners, who looked repulsed.

'Fine, then I'll just go to Mr Javanerd's office right now,' Benji said with a shrug.

'Jamie, take the wheel,' said Jenners. She **LEAPT** from her computer chair and towered over Benji. Benji's eyes were so wide you could almost see into his trembling soul. Jamie jumped into the chair and flicked through the CCTV cameras, desperate to get a glimpse of Barry Bigtime.

Then she spotted him. At 9.06 p.m. Sitting in a room making absurd faces at himself in a large mirror. The fires of rage began to bubble inside her. She gripped the mouse **TIGHTER.** She scrolled on. At 9.11 p.m., a round man arrived. He looked sad and frightened. Despite the grainy CCTV footage, Jamie noticed the man was wearing a cowboy hat.

Behind her came a **TERRIFIED** cry. Jamie spun around. Jenners had hoisted Benji above her head and was demanding that Mel open the IT room window. If a teacher arrived, it was game over. Benji was making so much noise, surely someone in the nearby classrooms would hear. Jamie **SPUN** back round. Barry was shouting at the other man. What were they saying? This could be gold. She couldn't hear over Benji's squealing and Mel's desperate pleas for Jenners not to throw him out of the window.

'MEL, I NEED YOUR HEADPHONES,'
yelled Jamie.

'Why is everyone shouting at me?' cried Mel.

Jamie picked up the computer speakers and pressed them against her ears like a pair of **LUDICROUS** giant headphones from the 1980s. Her mouth hung open and she closed her eyes as tight as they could go to try to hear the conversation. She could just about make out Uncle Barry's voice.

'*GOOD? THEY WERE FANTASTIC! They were one of the best boybands I've ever heard! They would take the world by storm, Winston, and you are LUCKY. You are lucky I acted when I did because if I hadn't thrown those chocolate-milkshake-sodden underpants at their stupid, lovely, talented heads, EVERYONE would be buying THEIR music! I need BNA GONE and GONE FOR GOOD.*'

Jamie missed the reply but then heard Barry again. '*I want. Them. Gone. Not just gone. Gone gone.*' Benji was **SQUEALING** like Sheamus did when Grandma pulled on his tail. Jamie strained her ears to try to make out what was being said but all she could make out was '*fed to sharks*'.

Jamie's insides turned to ice . . . **SURELY NOT.** Then she heard the word 'shark' again. She was furious with Barry, she was terrified for BNA, but she was also elated that she had discovered for sure that he *had* sabotaged them on purpose because he *knew* deep down that they were the best boyband ever! He was scared of them. **THIS WAS DYNAMITE.** But he also said he wanted BNA 'gone gone'. What did that mean?

Was he ACTUALLY going to feed them to sharks? Were BNA in real danger?!

All she needed to do now was download this footage somehow so she could upload it to YouTube and expose Barry to the entire world—

'WHAT ON EARTH IS GOING ON HERE?'

Mr Javanerd had burst into the IT room to find Benji upside down, dangling by one leg with his ankle firmly in the grasp of a **FURIOUS** Jenners, who was shaking him up and down like a yo-yo.

'JENNIFER. PUT THAT BOY DOWN. GO AND SEE THE HEADMISTRESS. EVERYONE ELSE OUT.'

It was too late. Jamie quickly closed the CCTV window and darted out of the IT room before anyone could think she had been up to anything suspicious. She had to try to warn BNA.

CHAPTER 14
FREE FOOD AND DRINK

Nobody likes Mondays, and it had been one **INTENSE** start to the week for Jamie. When she got home after school, she grabbed an entire bag of cheese twizzlers and her tablet and crashed on to her bed, too tired to even complain about the smells.

Jamie knew that if she tweeted BNA about Barry's threat she would sound like a loon or a troll. Desperate times call for **DESPERATE** measures, so she began to hack into the DMs of 2015's *The Big Time* champions, The Oi Oi Ladz. She and Jenners had sworn never to hack into DMs but this was an emergency so we're going to give her a pass this one time.

Jamie thought that maybe BNA would listen if the warning came from another band. She'd spent the whole walk home from school drafting how she could convincingly warn BNA that Barry Bigtime wanted them **'GONE GONE'.** The words still made her shudder.

The Oi Oi Ladz had very weak account security and Jamie was in their DMs with ease. She promised herself when all this was done she'd write an apology to The Oi Oi Ladz and explain it had been for the good of the music industry.

Jamie's eyes **NARROWED.** She'd spotted a group chat that made her cheesy-twizzler-dusted fingers shake and her heart pound. Jamie moved the tablet closer and then further away again, like parents do when they can't quite see the words. Shake District, Baezone, The Oi Oi Ladz and . . . BNA WERE ALREADY in a group chat? Jamie double-checked that all of the accounts were verified, her mind was starting to **EXPLODE**. The name of the group chat?

GP GARY PEPPER

Confirmed mate. Barry is doing it haha! HUGE party on Friday in a secret location appaz. The only clue is in this riddle.

TJ TROY JACKSON

Lol 'A RIDDLE' I'm too dumb for riddles lol. haha good old Barry, the man knows how to party I'll give him that. Bet there'll be good snacks as well so I'm keen tbh.

X XAVIER

You boys going to this HUGE party thing on Fri? also any1 got any clues on this riddle? Literally no idea.

NO NIKOLAS OLDSPIELLE

whats the riddle?

PJ PJ

You are cordially invited:
To the greatest party in all the land!

A treat for the world's greatest bands
The party will be held where your careers began
Come be part of my master plan
There will be free food and drink
ARRIVE: 6.30 p.m.

LL LIAM LUCAS ✓
FREE FOOD AND DRINK! AWESOME. Most important part of the riddle by far haha
what does 'cordially' mean lol. Apparently loads of big names going . . . and the Fenton Dogz 🙄

PJ PJ ✓
FENTON DOGZ LOL!!!!!!! Wow they've invited everyone. I feel less special. FIFA round Spence's tomorrow after studio?

F FABIAN 🐼 ✓
Hey we're in this group chat too. ☹

> **S SAWYER** ☑️
>
> SECRET PARTY!!!!! INDUSTRY AND STUFF?!!!
> :0 :0 :0 :0

And then messages that set off several siren emojis in Jamie's brain:

> **P PROUDY** ☑️
>
> whats the master plan bit? :S Food and drink though!
> I'm in.

> **S SCOTT**
>
> why are we invited to this? Lol

> **GP GARY PEPPER** ☑️
>
> Underpants band! You guys were awesome. Definitely
> come! Free food and drink. Probs goodie bags?

> **H HARRISON**
>
> Haha. He's arranged cars and VIP with us, him, head of
> the label and Baezone. Wants to 'apologise' and 'talk to

us about our future'. So weird. Never know, man, maybe he's changed his mind. I'm up for it. Free food and drink innit?

S SAWYER ☑
LADS DEFINITELY COME! RINSE THAT FREE FOOD AND DRINK LOOL

J J
I mean it can't get much worse than pants to the face lol, seems weird he'd bother writing that. It's from his actual email address. Maybe he actually is going to say sorry.

B BECK
Hmmm. Maybe. What have we got to lose, I guess? I'd take a sorry and a sandwich. Tbh I'd take a chocolate milk advert deal at this stage, I need to buy a new laptop. lol

Jamie had only been alive for eleven years but in all of those eleven years, she had witnessed a lot from Uncle Barry. Nine missed birthdays, defrauding her grandma of her home and leaving her solely responsible for a **CONFUSED** and **TROUBLESOME** pig, countless mentions of feeding people he didn't like to sharks and one humiliation of her favourite ever boyband. But not once had she witnessed an apology or any free food and drink.

Even without the CCTV footage, she'd know it was a trap. Barry was putting a 'master plan' into action – this was an **EMERGENCY.**

She took a screenshot of the chat and deliberated sending her warning message. Surely it would be too suspicious given how excited The Oi Oi Ladz had been about the party. She would have to reword her draft. The Oi Oi Ladz didn't seem to speak in proper sentences. But her mind was made up for her as an alert flashed up on the screen:

SESSION TERMINATED DUE TO SUSPICIOUS ACCOUNT ACTIVITY

She'd been rumbled and booted out of the account.

This was now an emergency situation. Two Valencian Four-Fingered Salutes in a week? Unheard of.

Jamie **LEAPT** from her bed to find her mum and make sure it was OK to invite her friends over again, but the only adult she could find was sitting in her favourite armchair in the living room, gumming on a banana and waving a controller around her head.

'What's all this running about for?' came Grandma's garbled cry as globules of banana flew from her mouth. **'Don't distract me now.** I'm break point down on *Mario Tennis* and Koopa Troopa has a mean forehand!'

Grandma made a whooshing sound and slammed the controller down with an 'ACE! YES! Can't return that, CAN you!'

Jamie briefly wondered whether Grandma was eating a banana for energy because she had confused virtual tennis with **REAL** tennis, but had more pressing questions. 'Grandma, can Jenners, Daisy and Mel come round now?'

'Sorry, Jamie, I can't have **any** distractions during tennis. Can't you just FaceTime your friends like a normal little girl?'

Suddenly, as Jamie stood there, a feathery flash of white darted past the window.

'What the . . .' Jamie said as Grandma fluffed her shot.

'THAT WAS NOT OUT!'

Grandma stood and screamed. 'You mushroom-headed excuse for an umpire. He wasn't even watching!' She stormed off and relayed the injustice to Sheamus the pig, who looked interested, mainly because he thought he might get food out of it.

Jamie turned from the window, went back to her room and set up a four-way FaceTime. Once everybody had joined the chat and positioned themselves in a room with suitable lighting, Jamie shared the screenshots that explained **EVERYTHING** she'd found out.

'Wait, wait, wait,' said Daisy. Jamie knew it was a lot of information to take in and she could feel herself getting increasingly **FLUSTERED** relaying it. 'BNA are going to a party thrown by Barry Bigtime? Have they not seen these memes?'

'I know!' said Jamie, aggravated. 'I don't even know how to warn them, now I'm locked out of The Oi Oi Ladz's account.'

'Maybe Barry is going to apologise? Maybe he'll

bring them back on the show?' Mel's hopeful tone was muffled because of the time she spilt night-time tea on her phone.

'Mel, that's stupid, you know what he's like. **He's horrible to everyone,'** replied Jamie, getting snappy. 'Exhibit A: I live with a pig! We need to find out where this party is going to be and warn them in person. Even if it means getting trains to far-away places on our own without grown-ups.'

Mel bit her lip.

'The riddle says the party is going to take place where their careers began,' said Jamie. 'What could that mean? Maybe where one of the bands played their first show?'

'Could be,' said Jenners, who'd accidentally put on the dinosaur-head filter without realising. She nodded like a very thoughtful diplodocus.

'Jenners. Look through each band's Wikipedia page, find out where their first shows took place, then hack the venue's systems. Email inboxes, online calendars, anything. Also see if you can get into the police database, see if they've been alerted to anything out of the ordinary happening. Have you hacked the police before, Jenners?'

'I have but it's **mega-risky,**' Jenners said casually. 'That's how I found out about that Baezone secret half-term mega-party in the city that one time. I can try while my dad's at the pub quiz?'

'Brilliant,' said Jamie, getting into the swing of this.

'Maybe the party is at *The Big Time* studios? It's near where I used to live in Birchester,' suggested Daisy. 'All of those bands' careers started on *The Big Time* in some way.'

'Great idea!' said Jamie. 'Could we hack their system again?'

'Negative,' said Jenners 'Never hack the same place within seven days of your last attack – that's a sure-fire way to get yourself caught by the cyber police.'

Jamie wasn't entirely sure the **CYBER POLICE** were a thing, but she trusted Jenners's judgement.

'But the party is this Friday – how else could we find out whether the party is at the TV studios?' wondered Jamie.

'My cousin Ronica could help!'

exclaimed Daisy. 'She's always at cool parties in Birchester!'

Ronica, a potential source of Daisy's coolness, was a **MICRO-INFLUENCER,** which meant she got invited to a lot of cool events but didn't really get paid for anything. She knew lots of mildly famous people, though, and even went out with one of The Fenton Dogz for a month for Instagram purposes. The story of their split bagged them a cool 1,000 followers each. If **ANYONE** would know about a party at the TV studios, it would be her.

'Amazing! That sounds great,' said Jamie.

'Oh, I know!' said Mel excitedly with her hand in the air. 'Maybe the party is at Barry Bigtime's mansion?'

SILENCE.

Now, we have to remember, it had been a difficult couple of days for Jamie, who'd felt a building sense of rage since the disaster on *The Big Time*, multiplied by the memes, in addition to Tobias Merryweather and the disturbing CCTV footage. It's simple anger maths.

'Why on earth would BNA go to a party at Barry Bigtime's house?' Jamie said. 'You really think BNA, Heartstoppaz, Baezone and a bunch of record label execs are gonna come all the way to rubbish Crudwell? **That's stupid.**'

'How do you know?' said Mel, **GLARING** back in a rare act of defiance. 'People have parties at their houses, even Barry Bigtime, I bet. Like my mum did on New Year's Eve that time,' she added.

Jamie was dumbfounded. How did Mel not get it? BNA lived yonks away, where actual music dreams came true.

'IT DOESN'T EVEN MAKE SENSE IN THE RIDDLE!' snapped Jamie. 'Besides, everyone was in bed by 10 p.m. at your New Year's Eve party. This will be a **cool** party, that you're not invited to!' Jamie's ears rang. 'Why don't you concentrate on finding that stupid goose and leave us to come up with a proper plan to save BNA.'

She'd gone too far. The other girls knew it, we know it, and so do you. Mel looked **STUNNED**, gulped, and left the chat.

Daisy frowned at the screen. 'That was harsh, Jamie.'

'Yeah, she was only mind-mapping,' added Jenners. **'We can't turn on each other.** That's what the baddies in films always want!'

'She always thinks everything will be fine,' Jamie said, reminding herself to focus, even as her conscience began to rumble. 'We haven't got any time to waste. I'm going to have another go at trying to get into one of the bands' DMs. There has to be something that suggests where this party is happening.'

Daisy and Jenners nodded, but Jamie couldn't help noticing their **DISAPPOINTED** expressions as they logged off.

CHAPTER 15
MEL'S VERY OWN CHAPTER

It had been a **SAD TUESDAY** in Jamie and Mel's friendship as they hardly spoke to each other for the whole day. After school, Mel was **DETERMINED** to prove everyone wrong and show them that she wasn't stupid, so had gone to find proof that the party would be at Barry Bigtime's house.

But . . . her hunt for clues wasn't going very well. She had been shouted at twice and almost arrested once. *You need to be more sneaky, Mel*, she told herself. The problem was that she was **INCREDIBLY CLUMSY.**

She'd got herself trapped inside a dumpster outside Tandy's Wine Bar searching for clues and had to scream until a very cross wine merchant hauled her stinky body to safety. When searching outside Super Larry O's Pizza Parlour for a lead, she was chased by a portly Italian chef who threw a meatball at her head and threatened to summon the constabulary.

Mel was sad, Jamie's words repeating in her head. They'd never fought before. They'd been **BEST FRIENDS** since they were tiny and always had each other's backs. *I will not cry*, she told herself, sniffing back tears.

When Mel was sad, she usually took a stroll in the forest. It was always full of friendly critters, much like a Disney movie. She was so preoccupied she hadn't realised that she'd stumbled further into the forest than normal. Being stinky, covered in meatball sauce, called stupid *and* now lost made this a contender for the worst week ever and it was only Tuesday.

Through a gap in the trees she spotted immaculately mowed lawns. She pushed through the tightly packed thicket and stumbled on to the freshly cut grass. She **GAWPED.** This was by miles the best garden in Crudwell. Who did it belong to? To her left stood the biggest house she'd ever seen. Was there a secret Queen of Crudwell nobody knew about? Mel thought about the biscuits the Queen of Crudwell could have, the lunches they would serve, and could you imagine the dinner parties . . .

Mel gasped. *Could this be Barry's mansion?* What about the iron security gates that everybody talked about, including Jamie?

They were wrong, thought Mel. Jamie could be a little too sure of herself sometimes.

It was the strangest garden she'd ever seen. It was beautiful but full of **UGLY** statues, which all had the body of a Greek god but a face that looked like an even uglier version of Barry Bigtime. Mel then noticed a colourful hot air balloon in the sky. She wondered if she asked nicely enough, maybe she would be allowed a ride in it.

Just as she was imagining waving to her friends from her balloon basket, she noticed a dumpster.

Clues! thought Mel and rushed over to investigate the garbage.

This might not be the first thing you or we would think, but Mel's brain works in **MYSTERIOUS WAYS.** The dumpster was big and after lifting the lid, she struggled to see what was inside. BNA would be so grateful to her for this, she thought. Into the dumpster she climbed. She landed with a **SQUELCH** in garbage

juice. The dumpster was stinky but sparse. All there seemed to be were a few bags and some boxes. Mel looked closer at the labels on the boxes.

GUGGLESCHRUMPF

Guggleschrumpf was an expensive drink, exclusively bought by cool people since it had gone viral on TikTok two weeks ago. Mel remembered the jingle: 'Guggle-Guggle-Guggle-SCHRUMPF, Guggle-SCHRUMPF'.

There was a dance and everything.

There must have been fifty empty boxes of the stuff in the dumpster. The people in this mansion **MUST** be ready to party. Proof!

Mel threw the box out of the dumpster for evidence and clambered out, then gasped at the tall, hairy **RAT-FACED** figure in designer jeans and a snapback that stood over her.

CHAPTER 16
ORGANISE THAT FUN

A particular difficulty when trying to plan the **WORLD'S BEST PARTY** is finding furniture that caters for a six-foot-tall man-rodent, a giant fez-wearing grizzly bear, three humans and a lobster-person . . . thing.

In the end, everyone just sat on beanbags on the floor.

'GREETINGS, CREATURES GREAT AND SMALL,' boomed Barry's voice as his face flickered on to a giant television screen.

'Thank you for coming . . . to this . . . our first meeting *dszhzz* of what is to be the greatest p— *dszhhh* the world *dszhhhs* SEEN!'

'Barry, sir, I think that cable's a bit broken,' Henrik said lazily as he opened his fourteenth pack of cheese puffs that day. The door to the meeting room burst open.

'RIGHT, forget about that, I'll just stand here and do it,' snapped Barry. 'Slottapuss, make yourself useful, you **vile overgrown sewage-dweller,** and take the minutes of this meeting.'

Slottapuss sat bolt upright, removed his sunglasses and started scribbling violently on to his notepad.

'What day is it again?' asked Slottapuss.

'Tuesday, you grotsack! Right. This party needs to be cool, *really* cool. The kind of party none of you lot would be invited within five miles of. I need ideas **immediately.** Flobster, your brain is a concerning, abnormal place – tell me five cool things **NOW,'** screamed Barry.

'Errrrr . . . fruit . . . oxygen . . . text messages . . . oat milk . . . Barry Bigtime?' Flobster looked up, pleased with himself.

Barry Bigtime stroked his chin as if he were solving a very complicated brain-teaser.

For future reference, when Barry strokes his chin it's usually a sign that he's coming up with something **EXTRA HORRIBLE.**

'Here's what I want you to do, Flobster. Do you see

the corner of the
room, just over there by the window?'

Flobster looked round and nodded.

'I want you to scuttle over there. Drag your
beanbag with you, put it on your head, stand as close
as you physically can to that wall and don't make
another sound for the next forty-five minutes. **Do
you think you can do that?'**

Flobster the lobster-man obeyed but as he picked
up his beanbag, his under-the-sea claws sliced through
the fabric, sending beans spilling all over the floor. In
the end he stood in the corner of the room in a puddle
of bag beans with the empty bag draped over his head
like a crab-ghost.

'Henrik, there's another multipack of cheese puffs
in the room next door for you if you can say something
less stupid than Flobster.'

'Well the funnest party I ever went to was
Fredericksen Hansen Christiansen Pedersen Smith's
party,' said Henrik with no urgency whatsoever.
Henrik had actually been to a number of interesting
parties. Barry would occasionally lease the bear out to

his cool friends as an amusing
sideshow. Fredericksen Han, let's
call him Mr Smith, was a wealthy Norwegian
businessman.

'Go on . . . quickly,' Barry murmured impatiently.

'Well, they had a DJ who was pressing all these
buttons and stuff and then went to the toilet and came
back four songs later. He was **definitely** cool.'

'Good! Yes, a DJ – more, say more.' Barry leant in
a little closer.

'When you arrived, they gave you food but it was
mini, so you had to have ten of them and there was a
place where you could take photos and send them to
people you didn't like, to show them you were **having
more fun than they were.'**

'Those cheese puffs are almost yours, Henrik!'
yelped Barry, rubbing his hands together excitedly.

'Oh and there was a chocolate fountain, but it
wasn't for eating, just for show.'

'Brilliant, *brilliant*!' cackled Johnny Whopper from
the truth-twisting team beanbag. 'And we could have
a hashtag! Or what's better than one hashtag? *Four*

hashtags! So *everyone* will know what an extravagant time we're having! Let's go for **#YOURENOTINVITED #HAVINGMOREFUNTHANYOU #PARTY4EVA #KingBarry.'**

Barry let out a squeal of happiness, before immediately trying to cover it up with a deep set of spluttering coughs, which made him sound like he was about to say something very important.

'Your cheese puffs are next door, Henrik. Bring them here – I would like one.'

There was not much Henrik would move for, but sure enough, seconds later he was **MUNCHING** on his favourite snack out of a bowl he'd fashioned from his own fez. His human ears twitched happily.

An audible sigh came from the corner of the room. Flobster loved cheese puffs.

'May I be so kind as to interrupt with a suggestion?' said Slottapuss, in a posh voice he was putting on to sound smarter. **'Have you considered chandeliers?** Really jazz the place up, give it a bit of class, you know?'

The truth-twisting team murmured in unison,

saying things like 'hmmm' and 'yes, quite' before Amelia announced grandly, 'We've discussed the idea of chandeliers put forward by Slottapuss earlier and we propose that to be approved!'

'Thanks, Amelia,' continued Trixie. 'We've also deliberated that everything should be sprayed gold and there should be **fireworks,** and the dress code is "designer chic expensive posh clothes".'

Barry began to smile so widely that you could see all the little bits of cheese puff stuck between the crevices of his **IMPOSSIBLY WHITE TEETH.**

Johnny Whopper chimed in. 'Thanks, Trixie for that mind-share. I was also considering a sort of Generation Z approach moving forward: if we get a ballpark figure for the guests, we could enable some innovative content marketing.'

There was a pause in the room as everyone tried to work out what on earth Johnny was on about.

'YES, get ten of those!' proclaimed Barry, who was now in a dreamland so vast, it was unlikely he'd ever find the exit and return to reality.

Slottapuss filled up an entire notebook of

suggestions, some of which he understood, some of which he pretended to understand but would google later, and some of which he was fairly sure were made up. *This must be what school feels like!* he thought.

Flobster had been staring at the wall for precisely forty-two minutes now. He'd thought about a lot during this time, including his **FIRST LOVE,** a crayfish he'd met in Barry's fountain, which didn't work out because of a poor work/life balance. He pondered on whether there was a cheese puff big enough that he could legitimately live inside it? He also wondered how Barry planned to get the ingredients he needed from his old boybands to make the best boyband the world had ever seen. After all, they weren't just going to voluntarily stroll into the **BOYBAND GENERATOR** and give up their prize quiffs.

Flobster still had two minutes left of staring at the wall, but this question was *very* important. He removed the beanbag from his head. **'Barry?'**

'WHAT?' yelled Barry.

'Do you think there is a cheese puff big enough that we could live inside it?'

CRUNCH.

Henrik clamped his jaw shut and kept his hand deadly still in his cheese puff fez bowl, wondering what was going to happen next.

Before Barry could explode, Flobster continued.

'And also, the party sounds good and all, but how are you actually going to get the boys into the

Boyband Generator?

Baezone's curly hair is unrivalled and you can't just pull off Scott from the underpants band's dimples.'

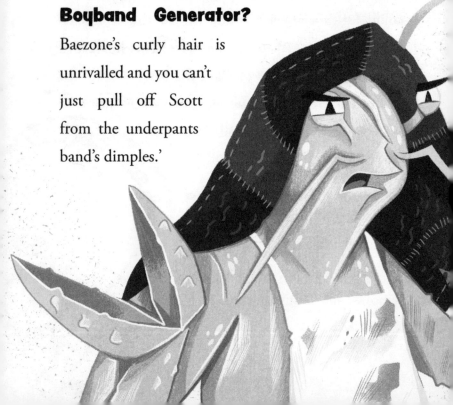

Barry's face dropped.

CRUNCH.

Henrik couldn't resist. Plus they were now made with real cheese.

'Well, obviously . . . I've thought of that, you idiot,' said Barry at double speed.

'Oh, OK that's good, I was just making sure because otherwise the whole party would be completely pointless, really,' said Flobster, as Barry **STORMED OUT** of the room like a five-year-old who'd just been told they're not allowed a lollipop.

Barry, you'll have noticed, had **NOT** thought of how he would gather the ingredients from the existing boybands. He couldn't admit that, though – he's far too bigtime.

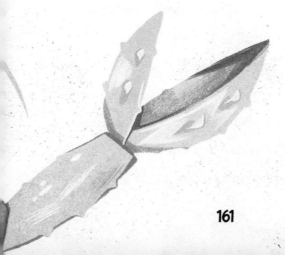

CHAPTER 17
TASTY PARTY BIN JUICE

Despite this minor flaw in the plan, preparations began straight away. Items for the party were arriving thick and fast, each one more **EXTRAVAGANT** and **OUTRAGEOUS** than the last.

Most of the heavy lifting was tackled by Henrik: as a six-foot-tall grizzly bear, carrying stuff was his calling. First, the elaborate glass aquarium to house the world's **ONLY** (and therefore best) octopus magician, who'd originally gathered fame when he escaped from capture, commandeered a boat and smuggled himself and other exotic animals across the Atlantic.

From the chateau roof came Flobster's faint shouts – 'Left a bit, down, yes you're almost there' – as he guided Bruce Burrell's Hot Air Balloon to the safety of the roof helipad. Delivering balloons by hot air balloon seemed a terribly impractical way to do it, but to be

fair to him, Bruce Burrell had been doing it successfully since 1995.

Slottapuss had found himself a clipboard. There was nothing on it but it made him feel organised and in control. **BEEP BEEP. THIS VEHICLE IS REVERSING,** came the sound of the first of a convoy of cement mixers. These industrial vehicles weren't filled with cement though – they were full of something altogether more delicious.

'Just over there by the side entrance, it's going in the fountain,' yelled Slottapuss, while pretending to scribble on his clipboard. He was really embracing the role.

As if navigating a hot air balloon and convoy of cement mixers wasn't a daunting enough task, Slottapuss, Henrik and Flobster also had to deal with the delivery people's reactions to meeting them.

'I've got a crier,' sighed Henrik as a small delivery man sobbed uncontrollably in the footwell of his van.

'A fainter here,' shouted Flobster, stepping over the passed-out body of a caterer. 'Three this hour – add it to the tally, **I think I'm winning.'**

Flobster's favourite thing to do was to squirm through the sewage pipes, up towards a drain, then pop up and perform a deep-sea crab dance, convincing the delivery person that they were in a strange dream. He'd watch them scream, faint or occasionally both.

It was almost five o'clock and Slottapuss had been working for a solid six hours now. He'd earned himself a tea break, which for him meant finding a stinky bin full of **DELICIOUS SNACKS.**

'I'll take the bin bags down,' said Slottapuss, and off he trotted down the gravel pathway, shaking the bin bags like you might do with Christmas gifts, trying to guess what's inside.

I bet this one has got some yoghurt slop in it, ooh, maybe even a fish head, he thought, *and then I can get stuck into the BIG bins!*

As he **WADDLED** down the garden, as only a six-foot rodent in sunglasses, designer jeans and a snapback can, he started to speed up as he saw the big bins. But then his gluttonous thoughts got interrupted. To the left of the bins, where the forest began, Slottapuss spotted a little human wandering up towards the mansion.

'Ugh,' grumbled Slottapuss. 'Why do delivery people *always* get lost?'

The girl climbed up into a bin. Slottapuss **GASPED.** She'd better not be nicking stuff. He ran over. The human re-emerged, holding a box. It was a girl, with messy brown hair and a brightly coloured sun hat. Maybe she was on work experience?

The human looked up at him and dropped the box. She rubbed her eyes, looked around, then back at Slottapuss and rubbed her eyes a second time.

'Oh, here we go,' said Slottapuss. 'What are you here to deliver?' he yelled. 'The octopus magician? More balloons, the disco goat?'

The little girl was breathing **RAPIDLY,** her face moving through the entire spectrum of emotions in four seconds. Then she stopped, stared straight into Slottapuss's sunglass-covered eyes and then:

'ARGHHH eeeeeeek brrrrraaaa!' she screamed.

And it didn't stop there.

'OOOOBblampfhghhBLAGOOBA WHAAAAT . . .!'

'I've not got time for this,' muttered Slottapuss. He lobbed his bin bags into the dumpster and jumped in afterwards. If he didn't have his break now he never would.

The next five minutes for Slottapuss should have been **GLORIOUS.** Discarded tuna tins, congealed egg remains, brown banana skins with little flies on, even a rogue rotting cocktail sausage. The real crème de la crème were the copious amounts of bin juice to wash it all down with. But he couldn't really enjoy the experience because of the persistent **WAILS** from the girl on the lawn.

He climbed out of the bin, marched over to the girl and looked her dead in the peepers. He removed his sunglasses, put his hairy little rodent thumbs in his eyes, waggled his fingers and went,

'BOO!'

The girl paused for a second and then immediately started again.

'Bleughhhwaaaababoooble!'

Slottapuss was stumped. He pulled out a pink-and-yellow-spotted walkie-talkie.

'Slotty to Barry, Slotty to Barry, come in, over.'

'You vile excuse for a pest, what do you want? **I'm busy,**' replied Barry.

'There appears to be a tiny delivery lady, yelling absolute nonsense in the garden.'

'I'm not surprised, if she encountered you. Take her to the cancellation pool and FEED HER TO THE SHARKS, then fill out the required paperwork saying it was an accident so we don't get in trouble.' Barry was **EVIL** but always did things by the book.

Slottapuss sighed. 'I could do, but there's a lot of setting up to do still. Shall I just eject her?' said Slottapuss, eager to avoid paperwork.

'*Fine*, whatever, just put her in the dumpsters and get on with it. I'm working on something and if you interrupt me again I'm going to test it out on you,' **SNAPPED BARRY.**

That wasn't much of a threat seeing as Slottapuss was literally a scientific experiment created in Barry's lab, but still.

Slottapuss shrugged, picked up the girl and tossed her into the dumpster. **HE LOCKED AND BOLTED THE LID.**

As the evening rolled into night, the **EXTRAVAGANCE** of the deliveries increased. An array of sparkling golden chandeliers, wrapped in extra-special bubble wrap full of premium filtered air from the Scottish Highlands. A complete set of organic marshmallow chairs for the chill-out silent disco zone, a twenty-square-foot claw crane game full of Labrador **PUPPIES,** an edible trampoline made of summer-berry-infused jelly. You name it, it arrived. At one point there was so much **PICK 'N' MIX** in the doorway of the mansion, Henrik had to eat some just to make way for the DJ booth.

With the lifting, moving and chandelier-hanging complete, Barry's team of oversized experiments admired their work, while being **WOWED** by an octopus that knew what your card was before you'd even thought of it. What a party this was shaping up to be.

CHAPTER 18
NitroJen08

Detective Lansdown's office was on the fifth floor of the police station overlooking Birchester high street. Today was the **GREATEST** day of this big city cop's career. He looked down over the civilians in his care, going about their day-to-day business, blissfully unaware of how much danger they had been in just hours prior.

He'd just defeated an old enemy, the Bean Street Posse, a **DASTARDLY** gang who would submerge their victims in vats of beans. But their bean-based atrocities were a thing of the past. They were locked up thanks to him. He didn't want any plaudits. He just wanted his streets to maintain their regular levels of mundanity.

He looked down at one of the kale smoothies his wife had been forcing him to drink since January in an attempt to tame his swelling belly. This was not a day for kale, he thought. If Batman had just defeated the

Joker, would he be spending the day dairy-free? **NO, OF COURSE NOT,** and today Leroy Lansdown was Birchester's Batman.

Detective Lansdown strode across his office to a portrait of the Queen of England that hung **PROUDLY** on the mahogany-panelled walls. She would want him to have this treat. He pushed her nose and the portrait swung open, revealing a secret refrigerator.

(We should point out that Detective Lansdown's wife was also a detective in the same building. She would occasionally snoop around his office, so he had to be extra careful where he hid his treats. Spies were easy to fool. His wife was not.)

Detective Lansdown had just cracked open a bottle of Choco Moo Juice when the door to his office swung open with a **BANG.** He almost jumped out of his skin, spilling his treat over himself. His partner, Detective Dubbs, stood in the doorway.

'Sorry, Detective, I thought you were my wife,' gasped Lansdown, trying to wipe the stains from his shirt.

'Understood. Anyway, hope you weren't expecting

the rest of the day off, guv,' said Dubbs with **EXCITEMENT.** 'Just got word from the cyber security team. An old friend of yours has just shown up.'

Lansdown frowned. Was he going to bring down two arch nemeses in one day?

'Surely not ... **NitroJen08?'** said Lansdown. To his disbelief, Dubbs gave a nod.

NitroJen08 was one of the UK's most **NOTORIOUS** hackers. They'd somehow manage to infiltrate the most sophisticated of police cyber security systems, with the national records of millions of people at their fingertips, but the departments they'd break into were always so peculiar.

Lansdown often lay awake at night wondering what the criminal must be planning next. He thought his cyber team was the best in the country and dreamed that he would be the detective to bring NitroJen08 to **JUSTICE.** He necked the entire bottle of Choco Moo Juice, grabbed his detective hat and marched to the cyber security department.

'No rest for the wicked, eh, chaps.' Detective Lansdown always liked to say something he considered witty when he entered a room. 'Our old friend NitroJen decided to pay us a visit today, I hear?'

As you can imagine, the cyber security office was full of computers and heroic nerds.

'Affirmative, sir, we spotted an alien presence on the transport record server,' said the nasally voice of the police department's best nerd, who they called

UBER-BRAIN. 'They're desperate for something today, sir, leaving locations we can trace. **Sloppy work.**'

Lansdown was cautious. It could be a trap. Or it could just be his day.

'This could be our chance, Uber-Brain. Spike them.'

That was nerd-speak for, 'Find out where this hacker is doing their hacking from'. Uber-Brain took the order.

'Sir, it looks like . . . It looks like NitroJen08 . . . is . . . There must be some mistake . . .'

'Speak, man!'

'They are . . . currently in Crudwell!'

'Impossible,' said Detective Lansdown – nothing ever happened in Crudwell. The most notorious criminal in Crudwell at the moment was a goose.

'Sir, we've got an address to a degree of 99.9 per cent accuracy.'

Detective Lansdown's eyes widened. 'Send all units!' he yelled. 'Dubbs!' he shouted at the top of his voice.

'I'm right next to you, guv,' said

Dubbs, holding his ringing ears.

'Get my detective hat – we're bringing down NitroJen08.'

'You're wearing your hat, guv,' said Dubbs.

'Well, get the car, get something. Get some bubbly as well. I think it's time we paid NitroJen08 a little visit.'

CHAPTER 19
R.I.P. GROUP CHAT

It was 5.30 p.m. on the night of the party. Jamie's attempts to crack the DMs of the other boybands had been far from fruitful. The closest thing she had found to any sort of clue was a TikTok of Stu from The Fenton Dogz posing with a can of **GUGGLESCHRUMPF** that was deleted two minutes later. *Did he arrive at the party super early?* Jamie wondered. With an hour until the party officially began, she was still clueless as to where it was taking place.

Jamie also felt a great deal of tummy sadness for being mean to Mel. Jamie had called to apologise but her friend wasn't picking up her phone or answering messages. Jamie felt **TERRIBLY GUILTY.**

Her phone buzzed. It was a FaceTime from Daisy.

'Jamie! I don't have much time,' Daisy panted. She was running and looked scared.

'Daisy? What's happened? **Are you in trouble?**'

'I did a bad thing ... Saw cousin Ronica ... Borrowed Mum's scooter without asking . . .'

Daisy's mum's voice boomed in the background.

'You took the scooter without asking like a thief!' she shouted. Daisy's mum Chandice had two moods. Ultra-chill. Ultra-mad.

'Anyway it got stolen, now she's about to ground me and send me to Auntie Dolores's behavioural boot camp, so I don't have much time.'

'YOU KNOW THE SCOOTER IS MY PRIDE AND JOY!' shouted Chandice.

'Party definitely *not* at TV studio. I repeat **NOT** at TV Studio. *The Hun Show* is filmed there every weekday until 9 p.m. Ronica's influencer friend is filming there tonight unpaid. She also said—'

But before Daisy could finish, Chandice had snatched her phone.

'GROUNDED. NO INTERNET. NO TELEPHONE. NO MACHINES.' And she ended the call.

Jamie knew Daisy wouldn't be able to talk her way

out of this one.

Frustrated and sad, Jamie joined her mum and Dominic in the living room and squeezed between them on the sofa. Her mum was reading an article about the **GOOSE ON THE LOOSE** on her tablet as Dominic watched the weird TV programme where you find out about all the football but you don't see any of the football.

Buttons the pug crawled on to Jamie's lap. She buried her face in his fur. 'This can't get any worse, Buttons,' she whispered.

DING went her mum's phone.

Sarah slid the unlock button and her eyes widened. 'Oh my GOODNESS . . .'

The last time Jamie had seen her mum this confused was when Grandma ate every banana in the house within thirty minutes of the weekly shop being delivered.

'Dom, look at this! I've got a text from Robert Tregland.'

(Robert was Jenners's dad.)

'Why is he texting you?' asked Dominic, trying to not sound annoyed about other dads texting Jamie's mum.

'He says the police have just shown up at their house!'

'What?' said Jamie in disbelief. Buttons barked.

'Must be a joke,' said Dominic.

'It's not! He's just sent me a photo! What on earth?'

Jamie leant over and saw a photo from the Tregland family's living room. What looked like an entire toy-box-worth of police cars was piled outside their house. Jamie's heart sank. *Surely Jenners hasn't been caught . . .* Things couldn't POSSIBLY get any worse.

DING.

This time it was Jamie's phone. Unknown number.

Hi, Jamie, it's Mel's brother. Mel's in hospital. We don't know what's happened. Found her in a dumpster. We thought she was with you. Hope you are OK. Give me a ring.

Jamie's mind was swimming. She felt **AWFUL.** Had Mel thrown herself in a dumpster because of what Jamie had said? Was this Barry Bigtime's doing somehow?

She leapt from the sofa.

'Where are you going, love?' her mum said. 'You can't go to Jenners's house now.'

Jamie took a deep breath and faced her mum's kind, confused face. 'Mum, I did something bad and I need to fix it,' she said, 'and I'm staying at Daisy's tonight.' She **DASHED** out of the door.

Jamie made it to the hospital in eleven minutes. (Helpfully for our story, everything in Crudwell was very close together.) She spotted Mel's brother (who, confusingly, was also called Mel) looking troubled in the hospital waiting room.

'She's gone mad,' mumbled Mel's brother, Mel.

'What happened?' asked Jamie.

'They found her in a dumpster, under boxes of Guggleschrumpf – you know, that cool-person drink that was in every TikTok video two weeks ago.'

Jamie nodded. All the influencers were drinking it even though it tasted like soil.

'She's saying she was stuffed into the dumpster and taken to the dump . . .'

'Who would do this?' asked Jamie, appalled.

'Apparently . . .' He sighed. 'It was the work of a **giant talking rat** in a snapback,' he said, looking at the floor. 'That's what Mel has told us, anyway.'

It was worse than Jamie had feared. It sounded like Mel had lost her mind. Talking rats? What on earth had happened?

'Can I see her?'

Mel's brother Mel took Jamie to see Mel. She was in a hospital bed looking sad and dirty.

Seeing her friend like this made Jamie feel peak awful. **SHE THREW HER ARMS AROUND MEL.**

'I'm so sorry for what I said. I was angry about Uncle Barry and I didn't know what to do and I . . . I didn't mean it.'

'I think I've caught the plague,' Mel mumbled as Jamie finally let go. 'I was bitten by a giant rat. It was huge and looked like the rats that gave everyone the plague that time, but this one was wearing sunglasses.'

'Oh.' This wasn't what Jamie had expected. 'It won't be the plague,' she said kindly, squeezing her pal's grubby hand. 'It's not the 1300s.'

They'd recently studied the Black Death at school. It was probably Mel's least favourite topic that she'd ever studied. The talk of **EXPLODING** black, pus-filled lumps had made her almost faint during the class.

'Also, I don't think rats wear sunglasses,' added Jamie.

'This one did!' said Mel, letting out a faint cough.

'But where were you?' asked Jamie. 'I tried

messaging, ringing, FaceTiming and everything.'

'My phone fell in bin juice. I was at Barry Bigtime's mansion, Jamie, I promise!'

Jamie scrunched up her nose in confusion. Could it be true?

'I know the party is going to be there, I just know it: there was a hot air balloon and weird deliveries, someone was talking about a magical octopus . . . I was looking for clues and found a box of **GUGGLESCHRUMPF** but then a rat wearing jeans and a snapback grabbed me and stuffed me in the bin . . .'

A doctor entered, checking her chart. 'That's enough fuss for Mel for one day,' she said, beginning to shoo Jamie from the room.

Jamie thought hard. She had seen Stu from The Fenton Dogz glugging Guggleschrumpf on TikTok earlier but hot air balloons, a giant rat? It sounded **RIDICULOUS,** it sounded **IMPOSSIBLE,** it sounded like a **WILD GOOSE CHASE.**

'Jamie, you have to believe me. You have to save BNA, **you're our last hope,'** Mel said, a little dramatically.

The Guggleschrumpf wasn't much to go on, but Jamie felt like she owed it to her friend Mel to at least investigate. The other option was to do nothing and let BNA fall into a trap. She looked back at Mel from the door and raised her chin like superheroes do in the movies. **'I believe you, Mel. I'm going to save them.'**

CHAPTER 20
Ain't No Party Like a Bigtime Party

The party was **NONSENSE.** If we normal upstanding members of society had pressed our noses up against the tall windows of Barry Bigtime's chateau, it would have looked more like someone had built a theme park rather than a soirée for musical colleagues.

Of course, if we were caught pressing our noses up against any of Barry's windows we would promptly be scooped up by Slottapuss and **FED TO SHARKS,** or if we were lucky, thrown into the lake.

The party was too **EXTRAVAGANT** even by Barry's standards. All sorts of oddities were dotted around the Brilliant Hall. Barry couldn't have just bought some conventional disco lights from the electronics store. Instead, the room was lit by living, breathing maned three-toed sloths wrapped in Christmas lights, who lolloped across a net suspended from the ceiling.

SLOTH-LAMPS were the coolest lighting trend in the world according to Johnny Whopper, who was probably a great deal happier about this arrangement than the sloths.

The Fenton Dogz were the first to arrive. Their eagerness to be included was adorable and **DESPERATE.** Wearing clashing brightly coloured suits, they'd proudly pinned on their name badges and signed a joint card. In fact, they were so eager to fit in that within five minutes of arriving they removed their suits and sat down in a big bowl of butterscotch pudding, because Barry told them it was on-trend as a joke. There they were, in their undercrackers, taking selfies in the sticky mess which was anything but cool. It was gross, messy and unhygienic due to the occasional added **DROP OF SLOTH PLOP.**

Kouros were marvelling at a sword-swallower from Djibouti, carefully constructing ten-second videos to show their fans. They were distracted by Sivan from The Oi Oi Ladz **FLOATING** past, with an assortment of colourful balloons tied to his wrists and ankles. He bounced safely against the net of sloths as his bandmates took about a hundred and forty-two photos and sixty-five videos of the scene, while everyone laughed heartily. It was lucky for Sivan that there was a net at this party. The last time someone got attached to balloons at a Barry Bigtime event, it was Billy Clarkson's sixtieth where one of Nica Konstantopolous's bandmates ended up **FLOATING INTO ORBIT.**

Roaming around the party was the only and therefore most famous **OCTOPUS MAGICIAN** the world had ever seen. His sleight of hand with card tricks was unrivalled, partly due to the fact that he had eight arms.

Playing the coolest mix of reggae, house and dubflop was **DISCO GOAT.** Headphones on, he'd occasionally look up from the decks to ignore guests' song requests, because his music was the best. He'd start every new song by speaking over the mic saying 'DIS-CO GOAT' and occasionally dropped rogue **FARMYARD SOUND EFFECTS** in the mix.

It was hard to tell if everyone was actually having a good time, or just pretending to have a good time for Instagram stories. Someone who certainly **WASN'T** having a good time was Barry Bigtime. He was wearing his best purple tailcoat and a purple top hat that had lots of tiny glitter balls hanging from the brim. Wrapped around the top of the hat was a rotating set of disco lights, blinking all the colours of the rainbow. He was bare-chested as usual. His legs were covered by pink silk pantaloons. It's almost impossible to imagine someone dressed so **BOMBASTICALLY** while also having a face like a **SMACKED BOTTOM.**

So why was Barry angry? Well, not all the guests had turned up. Four of them were particularly conspicuous by their absence. Those guests were BNA, and Barry's master plan was looking shaky.

Barry marched up to Johnny Whopper, beaming widely. 'Johnny! Quick word if I may? Perhaps in the quiet of the kitchen?'

Whopper knew that smile. It didn't mean the same as other people's smiles. He gulped.

'Of course, you bet!' he said doing a terrible job at

seeming calm. The two men marched in unison, both sporting ridiculous **FAKE SMILES,** careful not to alert any boyband at the party that there was any beef between the two of them. Boybands have an insatiable appetite for 'beef', 'tea' or 'trouble' as it's known to most people. They would feel immediately compelled to weigh in with an opinion on social media, despite having very little to do with the individuals involved.

Barry swung open the door to the kitchen, which looked more like a restaurant kitchen.

'Where are they?' demanded Barry, as soon as the door shut behind them. Johnny paused for around two seconds, which was probably 1.9 seconds too long. Barry was exploding. **'DON'T GIVE ME THAT NONSENSE, JOHNNY YOU GELATINOUS TAPEWORM!'**

He was so angry the disco balls hanging from the brim of his hat were swinging all over the place. He was so close to Johnny Whopper's face that some of them were bashing against Johnny's sweaty brow. Barry regained his composure, remembering nobody could hear the beef, or else the boys would rush in here like it was all-you-can-eat steak night.

'Where are BNA? They were supposed to be here at 6.30 p.m. **It is now 6.33 p.m.**'

'Sir, you are so right to be annoyed,' stammered Johnny, desperately searching for a way to defuse the ticking time bomb that stood before him. 'I'll get hold of Trixie and Amelia and we'll find out where they are straight away.'

'FIND OUT NOW!' yelled Barry. He looked for something to throw and spotted a delicious-looking roast turkey that had been laid out ready for the evening's buffet.

Barry **RIPPED** the legs from its body and started drumming them on Johnny Whopper's head. 'I. Am. Not. Going. To. Stop. Hitting. You. With. Turkey. Until. You. Find. Out. Where. They. Are.'

Turkey was flying everywhere. Johnny scrambled for his phone and scrolled desperately. It was hard to think while being attacked by turkey.

Meanwhile, Jamie with Buttons in tow arrived on the grounds. She'd popped home to collect essential mission items, and her *Adventures of Kid Ninja* costume that she'd worn last year for **WORLD BOOK DAY.** She'd promised her mum she was only collecting 'sleepover snacks'. The costume was so dark you could just make out Jamie's long red hair in the gloom.

Uncle Barry's chateau seemed even bigger up close. Jamie had only visited once before when she was very small. As she got closer, she could hear the distant murmur of weird electronic music and pulsing bass, and see flashing coloured lights. Her stomach began to flutter. **THIS SOUNDED LIKE A PARTY.**

Jamie excitedly opened her BNA rucksack and extracted her mission items. She tied her long red hair into a ponytail, then popped on her spy-man glasses and switched them to record.

She checked her phone. Harrison had posted an Instagram story twenty-two minutes ago with the caption, *'30 minutes until party time baybeee'*. If this was the big boyband party, it meant she had approximately eight minutes to find the perfect position to warn the boys.

Jamie had learnt from the Kid Ninja books that you had to walk with your back against the walls to stay hidden, so that is what she did as Buttons **POOED ALL OVER THE GRASS.** Jenners would have been proud.

Jamie edged along the walls and up to a giant, brightly lit window stretching from floor to ceiling. She cautiously peered in but couldn't get a clear view while staying hidden.

She popped her phone on to a selfie stick and turned on the front camera so she could look around corners. She quickly synced the output of her phone to her tablet so she could get a clearer view of the scenes inside.

What on earth is going on in there? thought Jamie, her eyes wide. The first thing she saw was a boy in just his underpants, covered in pudding and chatting to a dancing purple dinosaur. Jamie recognised the boy immediately. It was Stu from The Fenton Dogz. Jamie's breath **quickened.** *Mel WAS right all along! Does this mean she was also right about the giant rat . . .?*

She got down on her belly and crawled past the

windows like an army trooper. She popped her phone up every few metres, to get a glimpse of what was happening inside.

A boy was attached to balloons. An octopus was in a tank and it looked like it was playing cards? Were those Labrador puppies? **RED FLAGS** were flying in Jamie's mind. This didn't look like any party she'd ever seen on Instagram. Jamie got past the windows and used her selfie stick to look around the corner once more. She spotted what looked like the front of the house. Tall, thick, cone-shaped bushes lined the gravel path leading up to the mansion's entrance. These would be great to hide in. Jamie held Buttons tight, tiptoed across the grass and **THREW HERSELF** into a bush.

'You need to stay quiet, Buttons, OK!' whispered Jamie, wiggling herself into a five-out-of-ten comfy position amongst the branches. Buttons licked her face in agreement. Jamie was so glad he was here – she couldn't have done this alone. Now Jamie just had to sit and wait for BNA to arrive. Everything was going according to plan. **FOR NOW.**

CHAPTER 21
FOUR-EYED PUGS

Barry had been drumming on Johnny's head with the turkey legs for so long, there was no meat left on them. So now he was just bouncing naked turkey bones on Johnny's head.

'I'VE FOUND THEM, I'VE FOUND THEM!' Johnny whimpered, his greasy hair now even greasier as it was full of shreds of turkey meat.

'**WHERE ARE THEY?**' barked Barry, pausing his drumming.

'They're just outside the gates, look, Trixie just texted me.'

Barry gritted his teeth and pushed a turkey bone against Johnny's nostril. Luckily the turkey bone was too fat to slide all the way up Johnny's nose and into his brain.

'Bring them in here. Make them welcome. They are

our guests of honour. I want them having the bestest time that any of them have had in their pathetic lives. Do you know what will happen if they don't, Johnny?'

'Sharks, sharks, fed to sharks,' said Johnny, his voice sounding funny due to the turkey bone trying to force its way up his nose.

To Johnny's relief, Barry backed off.

'Oh, if you're lucky, Johnny. The things I'm thinking of would have you begging for a nice long swim with the sharks. Now go, I'm bored of looking at you.'

Barry let Johnny **SCAMPER** out of the kitchen, clumps of turkey meat dropping out of his hair as he ran. Barry washed his hands and untied two glitter balls that had become tangled in the commotion. Barry wasn't ready to **PAR-TAY** just yet. He had one more thing left to check.

He bustled across the dance floor. To his right, Kouros were having tremendous luck with the giant claw crane full of Labrador puppies. Liam Lucas had more puppies than he could fit in his arms, yapping and clambering all over him. You could smell the Instagram likes and dog wee from a mile away.

In the dining room, Barry found Henrik the bear dressed in a giant tuxedo, wearing his best and poshest fez, looking incredibly nervous. Behind Henrik was probably the most absurd thing any of us have ever seen in a dining room. It was a **SANTA SLEIGH** filled with hundreds and thousands of brightly coloured gummy bears.

Henrik assumed Barry had come to shout at him. **'Oh no,** have I got the time wrong? Am I late? Please don't feed me to sharks!'

Barry sighed. 'How could you be late, idiot bear? I'm not here yet! I'm the main event. I can't be bothered talking to you. Don't say a word again all evening.'

Henrik held his paws to his mouth as if to physically hold in any words that tried to escape.

Barry climbed on to the sleigh, trying out different poses for when Henrik dragged him into the Brilliant Hall and his master plan would begin.

Johnny Whopper was panicking in the hall. 'Must make BNA feel welcome . . . Must make them feel welcome . . . Oh my goodness, **I AM A WRECK . . .'**

Johnny was so distracted that he bumped straight into the purple dancing dinosaur.

'Oi, watch where you're going, numbskull,' came the muffled complaint of Slottapuss from behind the smiling dinosaur costume head.

'Slottapuss! Come with me!' Johnny grabbed the dinosaur by the wrist and dragged him across the Brilliant Hall, through the crossfire of Shake District's butterscotch fight and towards the entrance of Barry's chateau.

Outside, a taxi crunched along the gravel driveway. Jamie's heart was starting to **POUND.** Surely this must be BNA ... She tried to compose herself, rehearsing what she was going to tell them inside her head. She'd been reciting it since she'd left the hospital. Four boys began to climb out of their taxi.

'This is such a **dumb idea,** why are we going to this party?' said a voice that was definitely Beck's.

'I know he's wronged us, but it can't hurt to hear what he's got to say,' came the unmistakable diplomacy of Scott.

Jamie was starting to freeze. All her words were getting jumbled up in her head. This was her chance!

'I swear, though, if one pair of pants flies at my head, I'm going to kick off,' said J. 'Honestly, man, I swear he's just going to mug us off again.'

'Mate, this is going to be an **amazing party,** it's going t'be ridiculous!' said Harrison. 'It's Barry Bigtime! The man's a cretin but I bet he knows how to party, *and* there's free food and drink!'

Jamie prepared to **SPRING OUT OF THE BUSH** when she heard someone she didn't recognise.

'The men of the hour!' came a slimy voice. Johnny Whopper walked out of the house, arms outstretched, followed by a dancing purple dinosaur.

Jamie peered through the bush and bit her lip. Had she missed the golden opportunity? But before she could decide what to do, Buttons made an executive decision. He'd spotted the purple dinosaur and was very interested. **HE STARTED TO WRIGGLE.**

'Buttons, no, you need to stay!' Jamie whispered desperately, but it was in vain. Buttons leapt free and bounded up to the dinosaur. Jamie, in an attempt to claw Buttons back, tripped and tumbled out of the bush, landing in a **LEAFY HEAP** at the feet of Scott.

Eyes wide with shock, spy-man glasses askew, her face covered in bush scratches and her hair full of leaves, Jamie looked up. Jamie had dreamed of meeting Scott for a long time. This was not how she'd pictured it.

'Is that Kid Ninja?' said Beck, confused.

Scott knelt down to help her to her feet.

Jamie's brain was a block of ice. She'd forgotten her speech to stop BNA from entering the party, along with every word that had ever existed. She stood there frozen like the **SHOCKED FACE EMOJI.**

Johnny Whopper, who had the prospect of being shark dinner on his mind, was less than enthused about Jamie's arrival.

'What are you doing here, girl?' he said in that voice nasty people do when they're trying their hardest to be nice. 'Now isn't the time for autographs or selfies. Trespassing is very naughty and can get you into lots of trouble, so say a quick hello then be off – we need to get these boys into the party as quickly as possible! Television's Barry Bigtime won't be pleased if they are late!'

Barry's name jolted Jamie's brain to its senses. Buttons snarled.

'NO!' she cried out.

'It's cool!' said Scott. 'We can take some selfies here before we go in if you want?'

This niceness wasn't helping Jamie's concentration.

'Hey, can we get the pug in some photos?' said Harrison.

'This is hilarious,' said J.

Buttons was **GNAWING** on the leg of Slottapuss's dinosaur costume. This current situation was a disaster for all concerned.

Johnny turned to Slottapuss and hissed, 'Get rid of the girl, get rid of the dog, or we'll get rid of you.'

'Why do I always have to get rid of the little girls?' grumbled Slottapuss.

'Hey, girl, can we put your glasses on the pug?' asked Scott.

'Of course!' she **BLURTED OUT.** She didn't want to hand over her spy-man glasses, but this was her idol and if he'd asked for her entire head she would have tried to pop it off her shoulders. She handed over the glasses.

Beck had retrieved Buttons from gnawing on the dinosaur leg and the pug was mercifully nuzzling into Beck's neck and licking his face. J and Harrison cooed,

Slottapuss almost booed, Johnny Whopper was close to being **SHARK FOOD.**

With everyone else focused on the cuteness, Jamie charged up all her courage like a laser beam, grabbed Scott's arm and yanked him downwards so his face was close to hers.

'Scott, listen. You can't go into that party. **It's a trap.** I hacked into the CCTV of *The Big Time*'s studio and I heard Barry saying that he was going to get rid of you because you're too good at singing. That's why he threw the pants at you – he thinks you're the **best boyband in the world** so he wants you gone gone, not just gone! *Gone gone!*'

Scott looked confused, which was fair enough. Eleven-year-olds hacking anything seemed ridiculous. This was obviously a **SUPER-DUPER BNA FAN.**

'I mean . . . hacking? Really? That sounds a bit mad,' said Scott with a smile.

'I can prove it, Scott. I'll show you I can hack CCTV cameras!' insisted Jamie, pulling out her tablet.

'I'm sure you can, mate,' said Scott, still smiling. 'If we had more time that would be well jokes. But I've got to go into this party.'

Oh no. Jamie thought. *He thinks I'm mad. He's just being nice about it.*

'Wait, here's proof I hacked into the CCTV: before you went on stage at *The Big Time* you were doing the "Four Nights" dance in the corridor,' said Jamie triumphantly. 'If I hadn't hacked into the CCTV cameras, **how could I know that?'**

Scott's face changed. How *had* she known that? They hadn't tweeted or posted anything. They had been silent on social media for days.

'How . . .' began Scott, but before he could finish Jamie had been scooped up by a big purple arm.

'Time to go now,' came the muffled voice of Slottapuss. Buttons jumped out of Harrison's arms, still sporting the spy-man glasses, and began to bark.

'**LET ME GO!**' shouted Jamie.

'That's a bit much, isn't it?' said Scott.

'He's a fully licensed children's entertainer,' lied Johnny. 'That's why I brought him out here. We've had fans hiding in these bushes all night! **She'll be fine.**'

Scott looked unsure.

'DON'T GO IN!' Jamie yelled. **'IT'S A TRAP!'**

'Will you shut your mouth,' said Slottapuss.

Johnny led J and Beck up the steps to the party. Harrison was about to follow. Scott still looked unsure.

'What's the hold-up, Scott?' Harrison asked, eager not to miss any free food and drink.

'That girl thinks this party is a trap,' said Scott.

'I know, I was literally right next to you,' replied Harrison. 'She's hilarious. Did you see the photos we got with the pug in the glasses? **They're amazing.'**

'She said she hacked into the cameras at the TV studio,' said Scott. 'She said she saw me dance the "Four Nights" dance before we went on stage. That definitely wasn't on TV and we didn't post about it, so how would she have known that?'

Harrison **ROLLED HIS EYES.** He was itching to party. 'Maybe she knows someone backstage or something, I don't know. Look, mate. We'll just stay for a bit,' said Harrison. 'If anything looks weird, we'll bounce. Besides, there is free food and drink.'

'What should we do about the dog?' asked Scott.

Harrison looked at Buttons, who was still wearing the spy-man glasses. 'Do you want to come party with BNA? Are you the party dog? Yes you are, I think you are! Aw, you want free food and drink, don't you, boy!'

And with that, Harrison, Scott and Buttons **DISAPPEARED** into Barry Bigtime's mansion.

CHAPTER 22

The Pug That Was Also a Mole

Jamie was thrown through the air and landed with a **THUMP.** She was plunged into darkness as a lid crashed down above her. Her nostrils filled with the smell of garbage. She was in a dumpster. She tried to get out but the lid had been bolted shut.

She felt guilty again about calling Mel stupid when she had been right all along. Jamie wished her friends were with her and then realised Buttons was missing. Buttons, who was still wearing the spy-man glasses . . .

Jamie wriggled around in the dumpster, opened her bag and fired up her tablet. In the spy-man app she should be able to see **EVERYTHING** that Buttons could see.

To her surprise, the close-up face of Sawyer from The Fenton Dogz appeared on her tablet.

'Who's a good pooch?' he said in a baby voice before the face of another Fenton Dog, Francois, appeared.

'Maybe this dog could be *the* fenton dog haw, haw, haw.'

Jamie could see that Buttons was being passed around, but she couldn't see BNA. A sudden **BANG** startled Buttons, causing him to run towards a giant bowl of what looked like diarrhoea. *What kind of sick party is this?* thought Jamie.

Luckily, we know it was only butterscotch pudding, but through the grain of Jamie's tablet, it did look troubling. Buttons turned away from the pudding to yet another **HORRIFYING SIGHT.**

A giant grizzly bear in a tuxedo was dragging what looked like Santa's sleigh into the Brilliant Hall, to gasps of shock, awe and fear.

The boybands, who had seen many things on their pop star adventures, had never been in a hall with a bear before and many of them looked terrified. *Is this the trap?* thought Jamie. *Has Barry changed his mind and decided to feed BNA to grizzly bears instead of sharks?*

Atop the sleigh was Barry Bigtime. It looked like

he'd evolved into his final form. His head was flashing a variety of colours and his eyes seemed to have been replaced by . . . **DISCO BALLS?** Jamie would need to zoom in to work it out. Oh, no, he was just wearing a **RIDICULOUS** hat.

'MY ESTEEMED GUESTS,' Barry boomed. 'Thank you all so very much for attending this humble get-together. I'd also like to offer BNA, who were my guests on *The Big Time* last week, **my sincerest apologies** for my behaviour that night.'

Jamie was stunned. An apology? **IMPOSSIBLE.** Should she have seen some good in Barry Bigtime? Had her hatred of him clouded all her judgement?

'To say sorry, I have offered a gift to everyone here.' Jamie's view was temporarily obscured as a blonde boy attached to balloons floated past Barry Bigtime. 'In this sleigh are a special kind of gummy bear direct from Silicon Valley. These are magical gummy social bears with an extra secret ingredient! For every gummy bear you eat, you will gain a **hundred Twitter, Instagram and TikTok followers!'**

An audible **GASP** swept through the hall.

'These are my gift to you all! BNA, as an apology for the damage I did to you, please take the first bite. I hope we can be friends.'

She may have the occasional strop and maybe was a little too proud, but Jamie McFlair was not stupid. She smelt a rat. And it wasn't Slottapuss. Gummy bears that boost social media numbers? That didn't sound like a thing.

She tried to **TELEPATHICALLY** plead with Buttons to find BNA, but she couldn't see them. Why did all these boyband boys look the same? Then, to her horror, she saw Harrison swan-diving into the gummy bears, followed by Beck, and then the crowd of boybands **SWARMED** and mobbed the sleigh.

CHAPTER 23
BARRY GOES 4 THE WIN

Barry watched the boyband members **WRITHING** around in the mound of gummy bears with an evil grin. Usually in books and films, a hero arrives to stop the baddie's evil plan from hatching in the nick of time, but right now our heroes are either in a police station, a hospital, buried in garbage or grounded.

Barry looked over to Slottapuss, who was still in his dinosaur costume. The **NEXT STAGE** of his plan was about to commence.

As the boybands **SLURPED** and **BURPED** and **RAVAGED** and **SAVAGED** hundreds and hundreds of gummy bears, their eyes began to feel heavy and their legs became unsteady.

Troy from Baezone stumbled up to Barry with a glazed look in his eyes. 'Barry, mate, I'm sleepy, I might have to shoot.' He yawned.

'**Nonsense!**' said Barry. 'You just need a disco nap. Sleep here on the floor.' Barry hadn't even finished his sentence before Troy from Baezone was fast asleep.

Shortly after, PJ from Shake District, Caleb from The Oi Oi Ladz and Fabian, who was once in Shake District but was now part of the less successful The Fenton Dogz, were also asleep. Before long, every single party guest was **SLEEPING LIKE A BABY.**

Slottapuss finally freed himself from the head of the dinosaur costume, taking in large breaths of air like he'd been underwater, and hurled the head into the giant bowl of butterscotch. 'I thought I was going to die in there!' he spat. He was still inexplicably wearing his sunglasses.

'Shut your whining,' yelled Barry. 'Load up the carts and get these boys to the **Boyband Generator!**'

'Boss, there's a dog here wearing spectacles, licking the butterscotch,' shouted Flobster. 'He's so cute. Can we keep him?'

Barry yanked one of the glitter balls from his hat and hurled it at Flobster's head. '**I don't care!**'

Despite being an unpleasant human–lobster

monster, Flobster was not
immune to the cuteness of a dog.

'You can come and help Flobster take the boys to
the basement, can't you, you little good boy. You are
so cute, yes you are!'

Flobster, being **INCREDIBLY CAREFUL** with his
pincers, carried the pug to the golf carts, sat him in the
passenger seat and zoomed down the hall.

Barry climbed down from the sleigh and grabbed
Johnny Whopper. 'Have our extra-special guests
arrived?' hissed Barry.

(You don't know who they are yet, because we
haven't told you. But don't worry, you're about to find
out.)

'They're in position. The dad is down there as well
– he's signed all the paperwork,' said Johnny.

'Excellent,' said Barry.

Barry set off for the laboratory and arrived just as
Slottapuss was slinging a sleeping Scott from BNA on
to the pile of boyband members in the large brass
mouth of Barry's face.

Flobster sat holding the bespectacled pug in the

corner of the room as a tall, broad, blonde man strode over to Barry Bigtime with an outstretched hand.

'Cuthbert Merryweather, pleasure to meet you, Mr Bigtime,' he said, dripping with smarm and grasping Barry's hand tightly.

Barry looked at the four boys in the glass domes, attached to the helmets. 'Who do we have here?' Barry asked Johnny Whopper.

'Tobias Merryweather, Benji Leighton, Wilbur Lyons and Filbert Bennigan,' said Johnny.

It pains us to tell you this, but remember in Chapter 12 when Wilbur said they had been invited to an exclusive party to be turned into superstars? **HE WASN'T LYING.**

'Mind if I butt in?' Cuthbert Merryweather said. 'Sorry to be a nosy parker but can I ask, what's with all the sleeping boys?'

'Has he signed the confidentiality agreement?' asked Barry.

'He has,' replied Johnny.

'Wonderful, so Mr Merryweather is aware that,

should he disclose anything about the following conversation, he is liable to be fed to a marine-based animal of the shark variety?'

'He is fully aware,' confirmed Johnny.

'Great.' Barry turned back to Mr Merryweather. 'What you are about to see here, Mr Merryweather, is a **miracle of science.** Over there in that snoozing pile is every talented boyband of the last fifteen years. This machine is going to extract every piece of talent, charm, charisma and vanity from these boys into the machine and fuse them into your son and his friends. Then they will have all of the attributes required to become the biggest, **mega-monster-sized** boyband the world has ever seen.'

Leaving Cuthbert Merryweather opening and closing his mouth like a fish, Barry went to pull the generator's lever, but heard a yelp from the corner of the room.

The source of the commotion was the bespectacled pug. Barry strode up to Flobster and snatched the pug, staring into the glasses.

'I'm sure we could do with a little more cuteness in

the broth,' snarled Barry, carrying the struggling pug. 'Take these glasses, Flobster, they suit you.'

Barry pulled the spectacles from Buttons's face and tossed them to Flobster, who popped them on immediately and felt five per cent cooler. Barry then hurled the pug into the pile of sleeping boyband members, returned to his console and **PULLED THE LEVER.**

CHAPTER 24
THE BEAR

Jamie stared at her tablet in horror. She couldn't believe what she had seen. Uncle Barry was stealing BNA's talent and giving it to Tobias Merryweather? Was that scientifically possible? What had he just done to Buttons? The giant talking animals! Mel hadn't lost her mind. The lobster made her **FEEL SICK.**

Jamie's bravery faded suddenly. The sight of the giant rat had broken her. You know when you get that feeling in the back of your throat like you're going to cry? That was happening.

She pushed the feeling down. She had to escape from the dumpster and save her dog and YouTube heroes from her maniac uncle.

Jamie's attention turned back to the tablet. The spy-man glasses were now on the lobster, and his revolting antennae were flicking across the screen.

'Henrik, look lively – you and Slottapuss are on the night-time intruder watch tonight,' Flobster ordered.

To Jamie's shock, the bear from earlier plodded into view as the lobster continued.

'I think there's another girl in the dumpster who you should **PROBABLY DEAL WITH.** You grab the torches, I'll find you the crossbow . . .'

They were going to set the bear on her! The tablet battery gave up on the evening and Jamie was plunged into stinky, squelchy darkness. **SHE HAD TO ESCAPE.**

She stood up and rocked from side to side, again and again, until the dumpster began to tilt. With a final bruising effort she hurled herself against the side. The dumpster **TIPPED,** something snapped and she tumbled out on to the ground, gasping for breath. She painfully got to her feet. Now she had to find a way out of the grounds.

The dark gardens were lit only by streaks of moonlight cutting through the clouds. Jamie could make out the hulking silhouette of the mansion, and the looming woods ahead, with the foreboding bronze statues of Uncle Barry peppered between. She ran from statue to statue, hiding behind each one to check for Henrik and Slottapuss, hoping to make it to the woods unseen.

Jamie had never been much of a sportsperson. She hated PE, she always thought she was slow and uncoordinated, but it's amazing how much difference impending doom can make to your speed. Jamie gasped as a beam of torchlight cut through the night.

'Do you think we'll be able to keep the puppies from the party?' came a nearby voice.

'I'm still sad that we had to use the **cute little pug** for the boyband.'

Buttons! thought Jamie, choking back a sob. Jamie could hear their footsteps on the grass and held her breath.

'I didn't even realise we had a dungeon until Barry told us to put all of those **unconscious** boys in there, after the generator was done with them.'

Jamie dared to peek around the statue for a second and saw that the voice belonged to the tuxedo-wearing bear . . . His torchlight carelessly swept the lawns.

'Will you pipe down?' hissed Slottapuss. 'That's a top-secret plan you're blabbing about. How many times do we have to tell you? We don't need you out here broadcasting that the old boybands are going to be locked in the dungeons for a few months while Barry's new boyband get huge.'

'Sorry,' said Henrik glumly. 'There's no one here and I'm hungry. Is there any of that turkey left?'

The torchlight began to fade as the footsteps quietened. Jamie breathed out in relief. She leant on a stone bust of Barry looking like Hercules and gulped in air. To her horror, the statue began to give way and she was helpless as it toppled forwards and hit the ground with an **ALMIGHTY CRASH.**

She froze in the two beams of torchlight that spun to illuminate her.

'Hi,' Jamie squeaked, before she turned and ran as fast as she could. She stretched her legs as far as they would go with each stride, dodging incoming statues and leaping over garden ornaments until she reached the woods. She could hear the bear and Slottapuss close behind her.

Kssht! 'Slottapuss here . . .' he panted into his pink-and-yellow-spotted walkie-talkie. 'We've got a situation, category D, for Don't tell Barry . . . we seem to have an intruder . . . If all units could subtly move to the grounds with torch lights and anti-intruder equipment, over . . . **HENRIK, KEEP UP!'**

Jamie bolted through the woods, dodging branches, not daring to look behind. The torchlights danced around her feet.

'Henrik, use the crossbow.'

'I'm not using the crossbow,' Henrik wheezed. 'I only brought it out for a joke!'

'She's getting away!'

'She's just a little girl!'

Slottapuss snarled, snatched the crossbow from Henrik, took aim and fired.

The arrow whizzed right past Jamie's head and hit a tree with a **KERTHUNK.**

Jamie scrambled down a slope and leapt over a ravine. Were those the street lights of Crudwell twinkling through the branches in the distance? She bundled through a thicket and then to her horror came to a tall iron fence. She was **TRAPPED . . .**

She grabbed the bars and looked to the street outside.

She thought about her friends, she thought about her mum, Grandma and even Sheamus the pig. It was over.

Jamie turned around slowly. Looming over her was the hulking figure of the fez-wearing bear. Jamie couldn't stop herself from crying, but brushed her tears away angrily. She wouldn't go down **WITHOUT A FIGHT.**

'I've got her!' shouted the bear. 'She looks very delicious. I think I might just nom her down as a snack.'

The bear leant down and picked Jamie up even as she kicked and punched and scratched. **'Let me go!'**

'Stop,' he whispered in her ear. 'I won't eat you – I have a real problem with guilt – but if anyone finds out I've let you get away I'm going to be in loads of trouble so you need to promise me you'll never come back here, OK? Otherwise I'm going to be shark food.'

Jamie stopped moving, **SPEECHLESS.** She couldn't believe

what she was hearing.

'Quick, pinky promise, before someone comes,' hissed the bear. 'YEP, I THINK I'M JUST GOING TO EAT THIS ONE, OK, LADS?' he shouted through the woods.

'I promise,' Jamie gasped, wrapping the bear's claw with her little finger.

Henrik lifted her up to the very top of the fence. 'Careful! Lower yourself down gently. Right, now run!'

Jamie looked back at the bear from the other side of the fence. He had a **KIND FACE,** she realised . . . and human ears . . .

'Thank you!' Jamie said, before she turned and ran.

On the high street, a small car rattled towards her. It stopped and a window lowered.

'What on *earth* are you doing out here?' came the shocked voice of Mrs Bloggins.

Jamie felt relieved and ashamed at the sight of her teacher, who looked horrified beneath her leopard-print hat. How was she going to explain why she was running through the streets smelling of garbage on her own late on a Friday night?

'I need to go home,' was all she could manage.

Mrs Bloggins reached over to open the passenger-side door. After the dumpster, Mrs Bloggins's car smelt delightful, despite being an absolute shambles inside.

'Jamie, dear, you stink. **Where have you been?** What's happened? I'm really worried.'

It was odd seeing Mrs Bloggins outside of school. Jamie had never imagined what her teacher's life would be like after 3.30 p.m. She looked **MORE FABULOUS** than usual, beneath the concern on her face.

'I . . . I went to see my uncle Barry,' stammered Jamie, not untruthfully. There was no way she could tell Mrs Bloggins what she'd really seen. Nobody would **EVER** believe her.

As they headed to her home, she thought about BNA and Buttons the pug locked away in Barry's dungeons. There was no way she was going to leave them to rot while Tobias Merryweather became a star in a new band. Her fear was turning to anger. **THIS WASN'T OVER.**

CHAPTER 25
THE WORST EPISODE OF *THE BIG TIME*

THREE WEEKS LATER.

We'd rate the girls' current situation as a solid minus five out of ten. Things were **NOT** looking good.

Mel was still in hospital.

Jenners was in court.

Daisy was at a behaviour boot camp.

Jamie, after getting dropped off at home by Mrs Bloggins, had got the biggest grounding of her life.

CRISIS.

No Internet, no TV, no phone. Worse than the grounding was how upset her mum was that Jamie had lied about where she was going and about Buttons the missing pug. They'd promised to never lie to each other, especially considering how much bad luck their family had had with liars in the past.

Now Jamie couldn't tell her mum what had happened as she'd just think she was lying again.

Jamie couldn't leave the house and, with her friends out of reach, she hadn't been able to form a plan to **RESCUE** BNA from Barry's dungeons.

She was sitting in the living room with Grandma, who had her feet up on Sheamus. The adverts finished and Jamie groaned.

'Welcome back to *The Big Time* GRAND FINAL,' said the cheery voice of Will Kelly. 'It's all built up to this – we are about to find out who *you* have chosen to be this year's winners of *The Big Time*. Please welcome the first of this year's finalists, **4TheWin!'**

Tobias Merryweather, Wilbur Lyons, Filbert Bennigan and Benji Leighton bounded on to the stage. *4TheWin . . . Such a stupid name*, thought Jamie. *More like 4The . . . Bin.* Which was probably also where that joke should have gone.

4TheWin launched into a performance of 'What Makes You Wonderful', originally sung by The Lord

North Lads. It was by miles the **BEST PERFORMANCE** to ever take place on *The Big Time*, and by far their best in the competition so far. The vocals were flawless, the dance routines were hypnotic and the quiffs were hair-perfect. Tobias finished the song with three backflips and a triple somersault, landing on one knee with his fist plunged to the floor. The crowd **SCREAMED.**

Tobias and his band didn't look quite the same any more. It might fool a stranger, but Jamie could see the differences. Their hair was bigger and shinier, their teeth straight and blinding white, their clothes were too cool even for Daisy, and Jamie swore Tobias was now sporting Scott's trademark dimples. Tobias definitely hadn't had those in school.

'Can we turn this off?' begged Jamie.

'No,' said Grandma, the remote control grasped tightly in her hand. 'I've spent fourteen hours of my limited time left on this planet watching this show. I want to find out who wins.' Grandma looked wistfully at the TV.

'4TheWin are obviously going to uh . . . win,' Jamie

sulked.

'Hence the name,' chuckled Grandma.

The other finalists were a beatboxing double act called Sweet Cheeks, who provided beats using both their mouths **AND THEIR BOTTOMS.**

Jamie watched through eyes still puffy from crying as, after lots of unnecessary pausing from Will Kelly, Tobias Merryweather and his friends were crowned

winners of *The Big Time*. We're as annoyed as you are.

She'd failed BNA and her friends. Barry had won. As she refocused on the television, confetti was floating down to the stage. Wilbur Lyons was doing some bonkers breakdancing moves. This was a boy who couldn't even throw and catch his own apple a few weeks ago.

Tobias Merryweather skidded on his knees to the front of the stage as pyrotechnics **EXPLODED** and Barry announced that 4TheWin would be going to the World Music Festival.

This is a **HORRIBLE** chapter so let's end it here.

CHAPTER 26
A SELFIE A DAY KEEPS THE PROBLEMS AWAY

What a glorious morning, thought Barry Bigtime as he sat on the toilet perusing a rollercoaster catalogue.

He was glad of the moment's peace. His phone had been red-hot since *The Big Time* final with the entire world queuing up to hear from 4TheWin. Barry was **VERY SMUG.** He flushed, hollered for the house bottom-wiper and then jumped into his golf cart ready for a big day. Today, 4TheWin were starting their publicity tour by travelling to Radio Hun, one of the biggest radio stations in the country.

In the dining room, Barry took a big slurp of his Choco Moo Juice and banged it down firmly on the table, splashing it everywhere. Henrik quickly marched over and absorbed the spillage with his paw.

'Right, today is a **big day,** boys! Phones away, let's go through the schedule,' said Barry, slicking back his hair. 'The bus to take us to Radio Hun arrives in ten minutes. For the entire journey, you need to be taking selfies, or if you're not taking selfies, you'll be on the livestream. If you're not doing that, you're taking pictures *of* the livestream. Understood?'

'Yes, Barry!' said three of the boys in unison.

'Yes, B . . . oh,' said Wilbur a second later.

'When we arrive, there might be paparazzi wanting to take pictures of your darling faces. Smile until your face hurts. If it's not hurting, **you're not smiling enough,'** Barry instructed.

Filbert put his hand up.

'Yes, Filbert?' snapped Barry.

Filbert straightened his centre-parting with both hands and proceeded.

'Will there be fans there? Do we have to put our arms round them even if they look poor?' he said in a posh, slightly **DISGUSTED VOICE,** as if he was being asked to pick up a dog's bottom surprise in the middle of the high street.

It wasn't Filbert's fault he was so posh. After all, he'd come from a family who thought microwaves were evil and used three sets of cutlery to eat cereal. Sadly, this meant he didn't really like mixing with people who weren't as posh as him. He'd missed out on a lot of good friends, birthday parties and consequently party bags because of it, but he didn't know that.

'Yes, there will be fans, Filbert, you nincompoop. Put your arm round them, smile until you're in considerable pain.'

'**Ugh, OK,**' said Filbert. He lowered his hand quickly and accidentally squashed an unsuspecting fly on his plate in the process. He looked around, then quickly popped the fly in his mouth and swallowed it. Barry stared, puzzled for a split second, then **BLINKED** and continued.

'You are going to be interviewed by Nikita. She's important. *Be nice to her.* You've got one thing to talk about each – what are they? Benji, you first.'

Floppy-haired Benji snapped his braces, twiddled his multicoloured bow tie and said, 'The World Music Festival!' then posed, smiling, as if he was waiting for a camera to take a photo or expecting a dentist to appear and give him a lolly.

Benji was the clever one and he knew it, ever since the day he got moved up a year for getting an entire week's maths homework done in one day. He was also once the owner of the best virtual farm in the world on *FarmVillage*, which he'd had to delete because farming was now off-brand. Benji was the spokesperson of 4TheWin. His mic would be fully up for the interview, but mostly down for performances, as he was the **WORST SINGER BY FAR** (although nobody mentioned it).

'Good, Benji!' said Barry, pleased. 'Tobias . . .?'

'Talk about how great I'm gonna be?' Tobias sniggered, even though it wasn't funny. His blonde curly hair, double the size it used to be, bounced up and down as he laughed.

'Talk about how great the *band* are going to be, yes, Tobias.' Barry cackled. Tobias and Barry had the same sense of humour, which mainly involved laughing at how bad other people were or how great they themselves were.

'Your turn, Filbert!'

'How much we love our fans, even though some of them can't afford good trainers,' sneered Filbert.

'Don't *say* about the trainers, Filbert, just remember that inside your own brain,' Barry replied. 'And Wilbur, what do you say?'

Wilbur paused for a moment, deep in thought. Then his face lit up.

'NOTHING!' shouted Wilbur, overly loud and enthusiastically. All the boys laughed and Wilbur blushed.

Barry was taken aback, but not by the volume. Barry had noticed Wilbur's feet. A bulge seemed to be growing on his left foot, swelling more and more, like a water balloon stuck on the end of a tap. A big toe burst through his canvas shoe and seemed to be getting **LARGER** every few seconds. Tobias had noticed too.

'Dude, what the **HECK** is happening to your foot? It looks like it's about to explode!' he said, half terrified, half in hysterics. 'Doesn't that hurt!?'

Wilbur, who wasn't great with medical emergencies at the best of times, slowly glanced down.

'Oh my . . .'

But before Wilbur could insert a word not fit for books, he promptly fainted.

Tobias **IMMEDIATELY** got his phone out and started taking pictures, Boomerangs and even a selfie video with him and the foot. At one point he even tried to add a filter which would have given the foot a dog nose and ears, but it didn't work. Remarkably, the more photos he took, the more the foot seemed to reduce in size. By the end of his thirty-second foot-based vlog, Wilbur's foot had retracted back into his shoe and he'd come round.

Barry made a concerned and confused face, like a baby sucking a lemon for the first time. None of his previous boybands had had spontaneously expanding extremities before, nor had they ever eaten flies. Nothing like this had ever happened to his creations before . . . **APART FROM THAT ONE TIME . . .**

Anyway, these thoughts were spoiling his pleasant morning and he wouldn't allow it.

'Don't worry about that, he's fine, look. Probably drank too much pop last night, Tobias,' said Barry hastily. 'Don't post any of those foot pictures!'

Slottapuss burst through the kitchen door. 'Bus is here, boss!' he wailed, waving his oversized hairy arms in the air.

Peering high over the gates at the end of the driveway was the tour bus. It was almost identical to an iconic red double-decker London bus, except for one detail. It was painted with a giant Union Jack that stretched all around the bus, end to end, top to bottom. It did look **QUITE COOL,** although the paint was cracked and flaking off and there was a sizeable dent above the right back tyre. The bus looked like it had seen its best days twenty years ago.

'AWESOMEEEEE!' shouted Wilbur at the top of his voice.

'Cool . . . I guess,' said Filbert, slightly less excited. 'I'm not British, though – my mum is Chinese and my Dad is Irish.'

'Yes, well, I couldn't have exactly painted all of those flags on it, could I!?' snapped Barry.

In truth, the bus needed a new lick of paint and would have welcomed some new flags. After all, only nine per cent of their Twitter followers were from Great Britain – most were in China and Japan! But until he started making money from the band, Barry needed to be careful where he spent his coins. He'd got the bus from an old friend in the movie business, Gerald Hallwell, who let them rent it, his driving services included, for the competitive price of £83 per day.

Tobias, Wilbur and Filbert piled on, pushing each other out of the way while they did. Benji, who generally didn't get involved in such boisterous activities for fear of knocking his glasses off, wandered round to inspect the outside of the bus for safety.

Benji noticed a disturbing number of faults, including a small but continuous trickle of liquid sliding down the bus's exterior from below the fuel cap. Benji smelt it – **PETROL.** He gave a quick look around to make sure the coast was clear, and quickly sucked up the spillage with a straw he'd taken from breakfast. Suddenly the bus rumbled and spluttered into action, making Benji jump.

Barry popped his head out of a window. 'What on *earth* are you doing, boy!? Get your absurdly floppy hair on to this bus immediately.'

Benji wiped his mouth with his shirtsleeve, which smeared petrol residue on to the cuff. He licked it – **DELICIOUS.**

Barry narrowed his eyes. He didn't want to think about that concerning situation. So he didn't.

CHAPTER 27
Radio Hun

The narrow village streets of Crudwell were not made for large novelty double-decker buses. The bus **RUMBLED** through, steadily knocking wing mirror after wing mirror off residents' cars. One mile away from Radio Hun, Barry decided he hated the bus and made the executive decision to pull over and order an expensive **LUXURY TAXI** for the remaining three and a half minutes of the journey.

An executive, sleek black car arrived, driven by a man in a hat. Benji quickly nipped round to inspect the fuel cap but sadly there was no leak. He put his straw away.

As they pulled up at the famous Radio Hun entrance, Barry let out a little squeal. Some of the biggest artists in the world had passed through the Radio Hun sliding glass doors. There was even a plaque in the corridor marking Baezone's album *Peaks and Troughs* going **QUADRUPLE PLATINUM** in the UK.

Behind the red rope barriers stood hundreds of adoring fans, cheering, screaming and chanting, **'To-bi-as, come see us!'**

'I'm a bit nervous,' said Wilbur sheepishly.

'Ah, you'll be fine!' said Tobias, reaching for the door handle.

'Wait!' said Barry. He composed himself, ready to give his most wisdomous advice. 'Remember, what you are really feeling doesn't matter – it's what all of these other people think of you that's important. Just smile, keep smiling, smile some more and get in that door, understand!?'

'YES, BARRY,' said Tobias, Benji and Filbert in unison. Wilbur gulped and glanced down at his foot, which was throbbing again.

Tobias couldn't wait any longer. He clicked open the door handle and strutted out of the car, raising his head high and smiling at the phone camera flashes.

Filbert was next, but before he climbed out of the car he reached over Barry, picked up a dead fly from the dashboard and popped it into his mouth. He smiled, waved and reluctantly began greeting the line of fans shouting his name, as Barry's own smile wavered.

Benji took a big lick of the petrol stain on the cuff of his shirt and then stepped out too, posing for a selfie with the front of the line.

As Wilbur followed his bandmate, the throbbing in his foot immediately vanished as the cheers of his fans swept over him.

'That's enough!' shouted Johnny Whopper at the crowd, as he and Barry gathered the boys up, sent them into the lift in reception and pressed button number eight.

There was a certain excited energy in the lift, as all the boys except Filbert chattered about how much they loved the crowds. Barry couldn't hold it all in – he let out a small, **SQUEAKY** fart.

'Johnny, how could you!' Barry said, followed by an eruption of laughter as the doors pinged open, releasing the nasty air biscuit into the faces of the unsuspecting employees on the eighth floor.

There was something about
a radio studio that Barry had
always loved. With the slide of a fader, whatever
you said could be heard by **MILLIONS OF PEOPLE,**
pretty much anywhere in the world. Thank goodness
Barry wasn't a radio presenter as the world would be a
far worse place.

Thankfully, Radio Hun employed a lady called
Nikita for the afternoon show, an altogether more
lovely human than Barry in every measurable way. So
too were Nikita's production team, without whom the
radio show would be heard by a grand total of zero
million people.

Wilbur pressed his nose up against the glass of the
studio, the red **'ON AIR'** sign glowing inside.

'Sounding good, Rachael Lad-Adaygee and "Need
You" on Radio Hun. It's 4.34 and I see your texts and
tweets: the answer is yes, this year's *The Big Time*
winners, 4TheWin are IN the building. In fact, I can
see Wilbur through the glass right now. Stay where
you are, we're gonna chat to them after this!'

'What's her name again?' said Tobias, still buzzing

off his newfound celebrity status.

'Nikita!' snapped Barry. 'Don't forget, Tobias. If she likes you, she will play your song more and you'll have even more fans.'

Tobias's face **LIT UP,** imagining his own version of Jamie McFlair and her stupid fangirl friends fawning over how great he was.

One of the production staff gestured for the boys to come into the studio. Tobias pushed the door open with force, bumping it into the production lady who had waved them in.

'Nikita! I'm Tobias, such a big fan of your show, I think you're the best presenter on Radio Hun by far.'

Nikita had cool blue hair and a nose ring. She gave the lady behind the door a concerned look. 'Rayaan, are you alright?'

The woman nodded and **SNEAKILY** rolled her eyes.

'Hi, boys,' said Nikita, with a slight frown. 'This is Sally, who works on the show with me, and my colleague you hit with the door is Rayaan.'

Wilbur, Filbert and Benji all gave a little nod as if to say hello.

'Yeah, we can do a picture with them later or whatever,' said Tobias. 'I'm here to see you, Nikita!'

Nikita raised an annoyed eyebrow at Tobias.

Over the next twenty minutes, the boys answered all sorts of **IMPORTANT** questions from Nikita, like:

'Who is the most clumsy? Who has floppiest hair? Who takes the longest to get ready in the morning?' and 'What did you do to prepare for your amazing *Big Time* performance?'

Wilbur said, **'NOTHING,'** and everybody laughed except Tobias.

Because Tobias's attitude had low-key annoyed Nikita, she avoided directing any questions at him. By the end of the interview, he was visibly **UNHAPPY.**

'Well, we've got to know you lads a little better today, then,' Nikita said, winking at Rayaan and Sally, 'but now it's the moment your fans have all been waiting for. The first worldwide play of your brand new single! Who wants to introduce it?'

Nikita looked at Tobias expectantly. He stared back, in a deep, certified grump from having had **NO** attention.

Silence filled the radio.

Nikita's eyes widened, no longer looking at Tobias's face, but at his arms.

Filbert yelped, 'Errr, what's THAT?'

Nikita put one hand over her mouth and pressed play with the other, quickly sliding down the microphone fader. The band's single cheerfully **BLASTED** out of the studio speakers and out into the world. Inside the studio, though, chaos was unfolding.

'How are you doing that!?' Nikita said, pointing at where Tobias's arms had once been. In their place were two slimy, green, flailing **TENTACLES,** covered on all sides with sucker pads. Nikita looked to Sally and Rayaan, who were backing away.

Outside the studio, Johnny and Barry were pressed up against the glass, open-mouthed. Barry was sweating buckets.

Tobias was white as a sheet, the most confused out of anyone. One of his tentacle arms slapped against the glass studio window and stuck to it.

Filbert and Benji wheeled their chairs back into the opposite corner of the studio, now clutching Sally and

Rayaan like they were family members.

Barry said a word that's not even suitable for TV, let alone books. This was now a **GENUINE CONCERN.** His boybands couldn't just be flopping out their tentacles at a moment's notice. He thought back to Wilbur's swelling feet, Filbert's flies and Benji drinking petrol. What had caused these defects? Barry burst into the studio.

'Hahaha, we got you! Quite the performers, aren't they, Nikita! It was a **prank** for the boys' YouTube channel and visual content strategy! You got ... Tobias'd alright,' he added as one of the tentacles began to wrap around his head.

Nikita laughed nervously, a hand on her chest. 'I don't know how you're doing it – those tentacles look so real!'

Barry's phone bleeped. 'Boys, we're **TRENDING** number two in the world!' He started reading tweets aloud.

'*Your voice makes me melt, Tobias.*' And another: '*I've already booked our wedding venue, Tobias.*'

Barry looked up. Tobias's one tentacle had unstuck from the window, and the other began to unwrap from his head.

'*I HAVE to meet you, Tobias, you are my world.*'

As Barry read out more nice things, Tobias's tentacles continued to shrink. Suckers reformed into fingers and his hands returned to a normal shape. Barry wiped tentacle goo from his forehead and launched into showbiz mode.

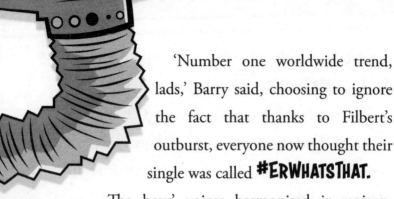

'Number one worldwide trend, lads,' Barry said, choosing to ignore the fact that thanks to Filbert's outburst, everyone now thought their single was called **#ERWHATSTHAT.**

The boys' voices harmonised in unison, marking the end of their new song, as Nikita slid up the microphone fader. 'Remember . . .' she said to the radio audience in a slightly more shaken tone than usual. 'We're also giving you the chance to see these boys LIVE at the World Music Festival this year, with five tickets up for grabs in our **HUGE GIVEAWAY!** Keep it locked to Radio Hun!' Nikita played another track and the microphone lights went off.

On the way out of the studio, Barry pulled Johnny Whopper close.

'Did you see those tentacles, Johnny?'

'Y-y-yes, sir,' stammered a petrified Johnny.

'Did you notice Wilbur's foot? Filbert's growing partiality to flies? Benji drinking petrol?'

'I did notice some of those, yes,' said Johnny, **'It's a problem.** I'm not sure why, but anything that seems to embarrass or . . . annoy the boys triggers these . . . **defects.'** Barry glared at Johnny.

'But why is this happening?' asked Johnny.

'DON'T ask questions. But good question, I don't know. Maybe reusing the boybands has caused a defect in the generation.'

'Like when you reheat rice?' asked Johnny, who'd once given himself food poisoning reheating a risotto.

Barry looked around for something to hit Johnny with but couldn't find anything so grabbed Johnny's ears and waggled his head for a bit.

'Understood,' said Johnny. 'What can I do to help?'

'It's very simple, Johnny. Do not let them out of your sight. Feed them with positive attention. Compliments, selfies, tweets, anything. They need to feel like superstars at **ALL** times. This cannot happen again or else—'

'I'll be shark food,' interrupted Johnny.

'DON'T interrupt me! But yes, I'll feed you to them myself,' said Barry sternly as they exited Radio Hun's doors, turning to smile at the queue of fans, which had tripled in size.

CHAPTER 28
TREES MAKE OXYGEN, NOT WI-FI

It was Sunday. Jamie was officially **UNGROUNDED.** She retrieved her phone, tablet and laptop from her mum, who clearly still hadn't fully forgiven her for lying.

The pang of guilt Jamie felt was outweighed by the fact that she could finally speak to her friends. Her group chat sprang to life and she was relieved to find that Mel had just been discharged from hospital, Daisy was home from boot camp and Jenners had been released on bail, but had an electronic tag which meant she couldn't be home later than 9 p.m.

Jamie

Guys, I'm ungrounded!!!

Daisy

Hooray welcome back!

Jenners

TOBIAAAASSS!!!! 💀 💀

Mel

I don't have the plague! :D

Jamie

We need to talk. Meet at Milano's pizza in one hour?
BNA in trouble.

It was great to be able to see them again and Jamie felt the **HAPPIEST** she'd been since the party.

But her happiness dimmed when she scrolled through her social media feeds. The Internet was full of people dancing and lip-syncing to 4TheWin songs. Everyone loved their crazy Radio Hun octopus prank. The hashtag #ErWhatsThat was trending at number two, under #MoneyCantBuyYouLoveFollowersCan, the real name of their new single.

Whenever Jamie felt a bit sad or confused, she would go for a long walk. She felt like she needed a clear head to explain to her friends the lunacy she'd witnessed at Barry's party. She glanced at Buttons's lead still hanging on the wall and wiped away a tear. **SHE MISSED HIM LOADS.**

Jamie tried to appreciate all the wonderful things about the outdoors, like trees, fresh air and bad phone signal, but her walk kept getting interrupted. In the window of the newsagent's was a homemade banner saying:

4TheWin making Crudwell Proud

Jamie looked away in disgust, only to see a pile of newspapers blasting the headline:

4TW: Winning in the Charts, Winning Crudwell Hearts!

Ugh! thought Jamie. It felt like she was the main character in a computer game where you scored points by annoying her. She thought about what she had seen at the party. Why was no one asking questions about how Tobias Merryweather and his chump cronies could pull off the best *The Big Time* performance ever within three weeks? She knew Wilbur and he couldn't even do a push-up in PE, let alone **A BACKFLIP.**

She walked into Milano's and up to the 'please wait to be seated' sign. But there on the wall was a photo of Tobias and his family eating pizza.

'You've got to be kidding me,' she fumed.

'For takeaway, madam?' said the waiter. 'What can I get for you?'

'Takeaway? Can you take away that **AWFUL** picture on the wall, please.'

The waiter looked puzzled. 'This one of Tobias from the band? They're local superstars!'

'They're rubbish and he's fake and they put my dog in Barry Bigtime's machine!' rambled Jamie, feeling herself getting worked up.

A few heads in the restaurant started to turn. 'You should be proud of them!' an angry mum shouted.

'Probably jealous,' someone else muttered.

'Jealous?! Jealous of them stealing talent?'

Jamie could feel her face getting hot. (Remember, she'd kept all of this bottled up for three weeks and everything was about to bubble over.)

'It's time you leave,' said the waiter, holding open the door.

On the pavement, Jamie breathed fast. She'd become so **HOT-HEADED** recently. She was just so frustrated that the meanest kids in school were being celebrated and that nobody was questioning their transformation. She'd felt powerless the past few weeks but this soon started to vanish as her friends began to arrive.

Daisy, looking as slick as ever, wearing a **LUMINOUS** green jacket and aviator sunglasses, immediately squashed some of Jamie's rage. She gave Daisy a hug.

Jamie's feet then left the ground as she was lifted up from behind in a big bear hug.

'I thought you were dead!' exclaimed Jenners. 'Look what I've got!' she said, showing off the electronic tag on her ankle.

'What's that?' asked Jamie.

'It's this tag thing. If I'm not home by 9 p.m. it alerts the police and I go to ACTUAL jail. My bedtime is technically at 8.30 p.m. though so the joke's on them.'

And then the icing on the cake was Mel, who trotted down the pavement towards them. She was wearing a daisy-patterned dress and leggings, a headband with flames on it and a hair scrunchie around her ankle. She and Jamie looked at each other for a moment before Mel's face broke into a grin and she gave Jamie a **HUGE** hug.

'It's so good to see you all!' exclaimed Mel. 'I wore this dress to celebrate Daisy coming back from bootcamp. I had a look for some Jamie McFlair-themed clothes and all I could find was this cool headband with some little flames on which kind of works.' She raised her ankle proudly to show the scrunchie. 'I got a grounded tag like the police gave to Jenners!'

Jamie promised herself that she'd never ever be mean to Mel ever again. She couldn't put into words how happy her friend had made her.

'Shall we find a table?' asked Daisy,

'We might have to go somewhere else . . .' said Jamie.

But within minutes, Daisy's sweet-talking had got them the **BEST TABLE** in the restaurant. Jamie launched into her account of what she'd seen at Barry's party: the Boyband Generator, BNA and the other boybands, Buttons, the talking bear, Barry's dungeons and Tobias Merryweather and his cronies.

'Who still says "cronies"?' said Daisy for the second time in this story.

To Jamie's relief they believed every word. 'I'm really sorry, Mel, I should have listened to you,' she added.

Mel beamed. 'That's OK. Thanks for believing me in the end.'

'This is getting a bit deep,' said Jenners.

'OK, Mel, please accept this slice of hot cheesy pizza as an apology,' Jamie said.

The girls laughed and Mel happily gobbled down the pizza, which reminded Jamie of Buttons, which made her sad. With the apologies dealt with it was time to get back to business.

'What's the plan?' asked Daisy.

'We can't let them get away with this,' said Jenners, squashing two garlic dough balls in each fist.

'Correct. *And* we can't let 4TheWin perform at the World Music Festival! They stole BNA's talents! They're talent-stealers!' Jamie said, her voice rising.

'Jealous,' said that annoying woman again.

'We need to do whatever it takes to get to the World Music Festival, stop 4TheWin and tell the world the truth. **We need to do it for BNA.'**

The girls agreed.

'One minor problemo: tickets are sold out,' said Daisy, twirling spaghetti on her fork.

'They're giving away tickets on the radio!' said Mel with a mouth full of cheesy garlic bread. 'I was listening to the radio in the bath, and they started interviewing 4TheWin, but I couldn't turn it off because I'm not allowed to touch electric things with wet hands, so I had to listen to it, but I didn't enjoy it! But they did mention that you can win tickets!'

'Ugh, they are everywhere at the moment,' grumbled Jenners. 'Did you see them on *The Hun Show*?'

All the girls nodded. Even though *The Hun Show* was a TV programme for bored grown-ups, the girls had all watched the interview out of morbid curiosity.

'I thought it was *so* awkward,' said Daisy.

'Also the prank with Wilbur's massive foot was so lame,' said Jenners with a mouthful of bolognaise that originally belonged to Mel.

The girls weren't wrong. It *had* been an **AWKWARD** interview, which once again, like their radio interview, had triggered a monster-defect. Unfortunately, Johnny Whopper was unable to keep Wilbur's bloaty foot off camera.

'Even Year 2s wouldn't find these pranks funny,' moaned Jamie.

'Well, we'd better win the tickets before everyone dies of cringe,' said Jenners.

The girls agreed that they needed to win Radio Hun's World Music Festival ticket competition to stop 4TheWin, which was not good news for their parents' telephone bills.

'OK, so how are we going to rescue BNA?' asked Daisy.

Jamie had a brainwave. 'It's Grandma's birthday next week. It's the one time of the year she visits Uncle Barry. I could go with her and then sneak off and find the dungeon.'

'Are you sure you want to go back there?' asked Jenners.

The thought of going back filled Jamie with dread. She also felt bad about breaking her **PINKY PROMISE** with the talking bear. 'It's our only chance of getting back into Barry's mansion without getting caught by one of his minions.'

The girls agreed, ate their food, paid and left the restaurant.

'Do you know what would be really funny?' said Daisy. 'If we got the whole festival crowd to **BOO** 4TheWin for some reason. Imagine how embarrassing that would be for them.'

The girls chuckled at the thought.

'Or better yet . . .' said Jamie. 'Imagine if we managed to throw a pair of chocolate-milk-covered underpants on to Tobias's head!'

The girls stopped in their tracks. It was the **BEST IDEA** they'd ever heard. It was the hardest they'd laughed in weeks. On paper, this was the perfect plan.

But you and we know what happens when the 4TheWin boys get embarrassed . . .

CHAPTER 29
FREE-RANGE SHARK FOOD

For most people, sitting at the top of a water slide would sound like a good time. Not for Johnny Whopper: this water slide led to the **'CANCELLATION POOL'** where Barry kept his prize possessions: three hungry tiger sharks.

Barry looked up from the poolside. He was furious about *The Hun Show* interview. Next to him stood Slottapuss holding a long hosepipe, with the nozzle aimed at Johnny.

'I tried to stop the interview, Barry, I swear,' Johnny Whopper called down, quaking in nothing but a pair of Hawaiian board shorts in November and flanked by Henrik and Flobster, who was still wearing Jamie's spy-man glasses.

'I gave you **ONE JOB,**' yelled Barry. 'To make sure the world doesn't see the monster-defects. And what do you do? Treat an early evening audience to a foot-based freak show!'

'I know, Barry, I'm so sorry, but look at the tweets! People thought it was a hilarious prank! There's not one shred of suspicion online! Look, I can show you—' Johnny tried to stand up but Flobster pushed him back down.

'Marinade him,' said Barry with no emotion.

Slottapuss squeezed the hose nozzle and blasted Johnny with a torrent of **STICKY BBQ SAUCE.**

'Look at them!' Barry said. 'This is what happens when the boys feel embarrassed!'

On the far side of the pool and now barely recognisable were Tobias, Benji, Filbert and Wilbur. The defects were getting **WORSE.** Tobias did not just have tentacles where his arms used to be – he now looked more like four octopi merged together, twenty or thirty tentacles all moving in unison, slopping gross **SEA-MONSTER JUICE** everywhere.

Wilbur still only had four limbs but they were at least twelve times as large as they should be, throwing him off balance as he tried desperately to stay upright.

His chest had expanded too and was muscular, his nipples the size of footballs. His skin was hardening like an armadillo's. He slammed his fist down, knocking himself over and cracking the ground beneath him.

Johnny was desperate. 'Barry, sir, please!' he begged.

'Shut up, Johnny, you irrelevant worm,' Barry interrupted. He pointed at Filbert, who appeared to be silently melting into a puddle on the floor. As they watched, the puddle started bubbling and rising. As it grew, it turned opaque and formed an oversized white speckled egg.

'Wait for it . . .' said Barry firmly.

TAP TAP TAP

Out of the left side of the egg popped the tip of an orange beak, poking its way through the shell. Tobias flung a tentacle towards a piece of shell, retracted his slimy arm and shoved it into his grotesque mouth.

TAP TAP TAP

The top of the egg cracked and a wrinkly bird head burst through. The creature was mostly hairless but with bits of yellow fluff stuck to its skin, a bit like a newborn duckling but **ONE HUNDRED TIMES LESS CUTE.** It grew rapidly. Now eight foot tall, it trundled off and began rummaging through the neighbouring bushes, eyeing up an innocent pigeon out for a stroll and gobbling it down whole.

Johnny screamed. Henrik and Flobster exchanged worried glances at each other (and you know that when these creatures think something is concerning, it must be **TRULY AWFUL**).

Slottapuss pushed his shades to the end of his long, hairy snout. 'Where's Benji?'

Barry groaned and whipped out a walkie-talkie from the inside of his purple suede suit jacket. He clicked it on. **Kshhhht!** 'HENRIK, get over to the limousine and get a selfie with whatever the heck Benji is immediately.'

Henrik, who could hear Barry perfectly well from the slide without the walkie-talkie, shrugged. 'Yes, boss.'

'GET. OVER. THERE. YOU BIG-EARED, REPULSIVE, FEZ-WEARING EXCUSE FOR A BEAR!' yelled Barry, his face matching his purple pantaloons.

Henrik did not reply but looked sad as he made his way around the house.

On the driveway, by Barry's limo, was what looked like a prehistoric python, except for a few essential differences. It had feathers, all pointing backwards along its long body. Its head was thick and pointed like an arrow, with two piercing black eyes. On top of the snake's head sat Benji's unmistakable **FLOPPY** hair. It was as long as the limo and half as tall. It slid up to the petrol cap of the car, rose up and pierced through the metal with razor-sharp fangs.

'Oh Crumbs!' Henrik said, slowly reaching into his pocket, keeping his eyes firmly fixed on the beast. As he did so he noticed the long body **PULSATING** – it looked like it was drinking.

Petrol! thought Henrik, being careful not to think out loud as he was known to do on occasion. Unfortunately, he fumbled and dropped his phone on

to the floor. The snake's head
rotated and its eyes locked on
Henrik. Out of its mouth came a **SLITHERING**
forked tongue which dribbled petrol on to the floor. It
started sliding towards him.

'B-b-b ... Benji, it's me, Henrik, remember?'
mumbled Henrik as he dropped to the ground and
grabbed his phone, desperately trying to open the
camera from the home screen.

It slithered faster now – ten metres away. Five
metres away. Henrik closed his eyes, taking pictures
desperately.

Snap, snap, snap, snap.

Henrik braced for the searing pain of fangs biting
into his fur. He waited, phone still outstretched. He
opened one eye. On the ground, on his belly, was
Benji.

'Phew,' breathed Henrik.

He scooped the boy up under his arm and returned
to the pool, where Johnny was still pleading with
Barry.

This is the longest shark-feed ever, thought the bear.

'No, please, Barry . . . I . . . I'm not even Johnny Whopper, I'm his identical twin . . .'

'Season him and **push him!'** Barry continued, turning away from Johnny Whopper as if he was in the spinning chair round of *The Big Time.*

'Close your eyes, kid. You won't want to see this,' said Henrik to Benji under his arm.

Slottapuss produced a sprig of rosemary from his grubby leather jacket, **PLOPPED** it on Johnny Whopper's head, and pushed him down the slide.

'Argghhhhhh!' screamed Johnny, his voice echoing all the way down the flume. 'I always thought you were a massive—'

KER-SPLOOSH!

There was a brief silence, a terrified scream, almighty splashing and lots of shark mouths **SNAPPING.** It was all too horrible for even Slottapuss, who had to turn away.

Barry gestured to Henrik, Slottapuss and Flobster. 'Now what have we learnt today?' he said **COLDLY.**

The three of them stared at the ground. Henrik sadly raised his hand. 'No more boybands turning into octopus monsters, snakes, birds and . . . I forgot what the other one turned into.'

'The points go to Henrik. Unfortunately, since Johnny's departure the responsibility for ensuring **THIS** does not happen again lies with you three. If one of you fails, **you all fail** and, if you ask me, the sharks look like they're ready for a pudding.'

Barry swept away as Flobster, Henrik and Slottapuss dealt out the necessary amounts of attention and compliments to turn Tobias, Filbert and Wilbur back into their normal selves.

CHAPTER 30
GRANDMA'S BIRTHDAY BREAKOUT

It was Grandma's birthday and Jamie was already feeling ill at the prospect of returning to Uncle Barry's mansion. Although every time she felt scared, she pictured Tobias Merryweather being **HIT IN THE FACE WITH PANTS** at the World Music Festival. *It's SUCH a good plan*, she thought.

For this visit to Uncle Barry's she was far more prepared. She'd spent hours watching YouTube tutorials on how to construct the tools she needed to bust BNA from the dungeon and to take care of any giant rats. She packed the supplies in her BNA backpack.

As for part two of the plan, Jenners, Jamie and Daisy had taken it in turns to stay on hold on their parents' phones to try to win tickets to the **WORLD MUSIC FESTIVAL** but to no avail. For most of them it was the first time they had ever used the house phone.

Time was running out and now it was Mel's turn. She'd been trying to get through to the competition line for a whole hour, when suddenly, 'Hello, you're through to Radio Hun.' Mel's heart leapt. 'Hi, who's there, please?' said the voice.

Mel panicked. **'Hello . . . It's Muh— Muh—'**

'OK then, Mo-Mo, have you read the terms and conditions online?' said the voice on the other end.

Now all of us reading this know that neither Mel nor the person she was speaking to had read a single term or condition on the website, but that was **NOT** about to stop her going to the World Music Festival.

'Yes!' lied Mel, who for once didn't feel at all bad.

'Great, and are you over eighteen?'

'I sure am, fellow grown-up!' said Mel. *No more lies after this phone call*, she promised herself.

'Great, the next voice you'll hear will be Nikita's. **Good luck!'**

Occasionally there are moments in your life where you cannot afford to slip up. School sports day, asking parents if your friend can stay for a sleepover, persuading a grown-up you are responsible enough to own a dog. **THIS WAS ONE OF THESE MOMENTS . . .** and Mel had already got her own name wrong.

'This is Nikita on Radio Hun, competition time once again,' came the familiar voice. 'One lucky winner will take our five final sold-out tickets to the World Music Festival! One question stands in your way. On the line we have . . . Mo-Mo!'

'Hello!' Mel said nervously, as tense music played in the background.

'Good luck, Mo-Mo, here comes your question. Barry Bigtime is known as many things: the King of the Boybands, the Sultan of Sound and the Prince of Pop . . . **But what is Barry Bigtime's real name?'** Nikita started the beeping countdown.

'*Real* name?' Mel was so confused. Jamie would know. But Jamie called him Uncle Barry. Everyone called him Barry. Apart from Jenners. But she couldn't use that name. The Internet would know! She stretched for her phone. But her house phone was ancient and was connected to the wall by a cord.

'We need an answer, please, Mo-Mo!'

What if it was a trick question? That was it! Surely it was just . . .

' . . . Barry Bigtime?'

WROOONG!

'*Ooh*, so close,' came the reply. 'Wrong answer, I'm afraid. The question rolls over to our next entrant on line two. Can they win the last remaining tickets? Hello, **Mabel McDonaldore?**'

Mel's heart sank. She was so close; the girls would be so disappointed . . .

WAIT a minute! Mabel McDonaldore . . . why does that name ring a bell?

In her kitchen, Jamie stood by the radio with her head in hands. Their golden opportunity had slipped away from them. She couldn't be mad at Mel, though. One, because she'd promised herself she never would be again, and two, it was a really hard question. She'd briefly forgotten the answer herself. She'd always called him Uncle Barry.

'Psst! I'm about to light the candles on Grandma's

birthday cake!' hissed Jamie's mum with a **SMILE.** Things were still difficult between them since the grounding and Jamie hoped this meant it was getting better.

Jamie zoned out from the radio as they sneakily prepared the candles. Grandma had blown out the candles on over eighty birthday cakes in her time. This one was probably not going to come as a shock. To Jamie's surprise, though, she heard Grandma's voice. Had she spoilt her unsurprising birthday cake surprise by bundling in unannounced? But she wasn't in the kitchen. The voice was coming from the radio.

'CONGRATULATIONS, MABEL!' shouted Nikita, as celebratory fanfare blasted out of the speakers. **'PACK YOUR BAGS,** because TOMORROW you're heading to the World Music Festival!'

Surely not. That couldn't be Grandma. Jamie ran to her bedroom and found Grandma on her mobile, celebrating wildly, jumping up and down on the bed.

'Grandma, you won!?' Jamie couldn't believe it.

Jamie's mum came in too and the three of them

hugged. Sarah shook her head in disbelief. 'Who are you going to take with you, Mum?' she said, tilting her head towards Jamie.

'Please take me with you!' begged Jamie.

'Sorry, Jamie, you've got plenty of World Music Festivals in your future. For us old girls, every day above ground is a bonus. We could be dead tomorrow!'

Jamie thought hard. 'But . . . But . . . aren't we going to see Uncle Barry tomorrow? What if you don't make the festival in time?'

'I'll have plenty of time to do both,' said Grandma. With that she gleefully rode her stairlift up to the bathroom, as the excitement had triggered a **BOWEL MOVEMENT.**

Jamie bit her bottom lip; they *needed* those festival tickets!

Jamie opened FaceTime to find an inconsolable Mel being comforted by Daisy and Jenners. Jamie shared her bad news.

'. . . and then she said her friends could be dead tomorrow,' finished Jamie.

'Only one thing for it, then,' said Jenners. **'Take. Down. Those . . . GRANNIES!'**

'Jenners, we're not assassins,' said Daisy.

'Not like ACTUALLY take them out . . .' Jenners explained, 'but just keep them occupied with something else for the day.'

The group chat went silent as the three other girls desperately tried to think of a better plan.

'See, it's our only option. Jamie, you keep your Grandma busy at Uncle Barry's and deal with rescuing BNA and Buttons. Me, Daisy and Mel will meet first thing tomorrow to commence operation Granny Takedown. We'll have BNA out of the dungeons and heading to the World Music Festival before Barry even knows what's going on.'

CHAPTER 31

THE BOYBAND DUNGEON

The next day was cold and blustery. Jamie clung to Grandma for dear life. She had no idea that mobility scooters could reach such speeds. Grandma could barely see, hear or remember her own name but she was **UNAFRAID** of putting pedal to the metal.

'There's a lovely boy who always looks after me at your Uncle Barry's every year,' said Grandma, turning around to Jamie with a twinkle in her eye.

'Oh, that sounds nice, Grandma,' said Jamie. She desperately didn't want to hear any more details and she also wanted Grandma to keep her eyes on the road.

'He's a bit of me,' the old lady said with a wink. **'Johnny Whopper's his name.'**

Uncle Barry's mansion soon loomed into view. Jamie felt Grandma's leftover birthday cake shift uncomfortably in her stomach. She wasn't alone this time, though – her friends were part of the plan.

As the security entrance gates slid open, they were collected by a smartly dressed lady who looked like she'd been up all night watching horror movies. Grandma looked at the woman as if she were the contents of a sneezed-on handkerchief.

'Who on earth are you?' asked Grandma, in a way that some people might not consider polite. 'Where's my Johnny?'

The lady shifted uncomfortably. 'Johnny's, uh . . . he's at a **special lunch** today. I'm Trixie and I've been instructed to ask if you've taken your medicine this morning?'

'Yes, yes, girl, of course I have, **I'm not stupid.**'

'Wonderful . . . now . . . I can only apologise that Johnny isn't here to greet you . . . He's . . .' Trixie looked at the open gates, her eyes darting wildly. To Jamie and Grandma's surprise, Trixie sprinted past them, **OUT OF THE GATE** and down the street.

'Whatever next!?' gasped Grandma. 'How awfully rude.'

Jamie wondered if she'd be running

again soon too.

Grandma's scooter accelerated up the gravel path, up the disability ramp and into the great foyer. Jamie sent a quick update to her group chat to let them know she'd successfully infiltrated the mansion.

The massive room was **EERILY** silent apart from the tinkle of the Barry fountain and the shuffling of housekeepers. Jamie clung to Grandma's waist as the scooter tootled through the great halls of the chateau. Her brain struggled to absorb the **RIDICULOUSNESS** of the mansion decor. *Everything is killing me with cringe*, she thought as she looked around.

From the paintings of her uncle Barry depicted as various musclebound characters, to the tapestries emblazoned with slogans such as *Stuff = Happiness* and *Everyone is legitimately worse than Barry Bigtime – Gandhi*, **EVERYTHING WAS AWFUL.**

The excess made her think of Scott from BNA's struggles to even get the chance to make music. It made her even more determined to bust her favourite band out of the dungeon they were trapped in.

Grandma and Jamie pulled into a second lobby.

The room was round with several corridors spreading in different directions like spiders' legs. Jamie's mouth fell open. The centrepiece of the room was the most bewildering statue of Uncle Barry yet.

'This one's a new one, my word,' said Grandma.

The statue looked like Uncle Barry had been **FUSED WITH AN OCTOPUS.** His stone face grinned maniacally as long tentacles of marble snaked in all directions. Each tentacle was clutching a golden rabbit with a silver carrot in its paws. Jamie didn't want to think what all of this may symbolise and if for some reason you're studying this story for school, I wouldn't dig too deep either.

Jamie climbed off the scooter and looked around. The face of the **OCTOBARRY** made her insides feel cold. The frightened faces of the rabbits made her feel worse. But wait, what was that?

She looked closer and saw that one of the carrots had *Pool* written on it. She looked at the other carrots. One said *Brilliant Hall*, another said *Toilets* and one said . . .

'DUNGEONS!' exclaimed Jamie.

'Dungeons? Have you been on the silly juice, girl? We need to get to the Brilliant Hall. I've only got thirty minutes with my firstborn, I can't be late!'

'Grandma, the Brilliant Hall is down that way,' said Jamie, pointing. 'This statue thing is a signpost.'

Grandma didn't look convinced because, let's be fair, that is **MAD.** She raised an eyebrow. 'Well, if you're sure, Jamie. Saddle up, this may be a bumpy ride!'

'Grandma . . . I need the toilet, actually. I'll catch you up.'

'I can't leave you in this ridiculous place, Jamie. By the time you find your way out you'll be older than me.'

'I think I've got a **REALLY** upset stomach, Grandma,' said Jamie.

Grandma's eyes widened.

'OK, do what you have to do!' relented Grandma. 'I can't deal with you soiling yourself over my birthday cardigan. I'll see you at the lunch.' With that, Grandma sped away, straight into a housekeeper, who bounced off the front of the scooter and into a suit of armour that collapsed on top of their flailing body.

Once Grandma was out of sight, Jamie set off down the corridor the dungeon carrot pointed to. Now she was alone, it was time to get prepared. She checked for signs of staff members, human or otherwise, and swung open her backpack.

Jamie's first weapon was a set of fun-sized bottles of cola, pre-mixed with Mentos that, when thrown – according to a YouTube tutorial – would cause a devastating yet **DELICIOUS EXPLOSION.** Each bottle was attached to a pink *Magaluf 09* sash that she'd stolen from her mum. She fastened the sash of sugary grenades over her shoulder.

She then pulled out two water pistols filled with a cocktail of bin juice, itching powder and Grandma's perfume. She placed them into holsters that she'd fashioned from an old yellow judo belt and tied it around her waist.

Finally, she locked and loaded a **MEGASOAKER 4000** that she'd modified into a slime blaster. She'd filled the blaster with an EXTRA-STICKY SLIME recipe that she'd learnt from top SlimeTuber GooeyBallooey. The tutorial had over 150,000 likes so it was bound to be **AWESOME.**

After a dizzying amount of turns in the corridor, the dungeon entrance came into view. Two statues of Barry riding a serpent stood either side of a large stone arch. The door was exactly like a dungeon you'd find in a castle, a hulking grid of thick black iron.

A ridiculously big lock barred her way. Yet Jamie was unmoved. She hadn't sat through three hours of tutorials on lock-picking for nothing. She pulled a clip from her hair and got to work. The padlock **SNAPPED OPEN** with a click.

Jamie took a deep breath and pushed her shoulder against the heavy iron door with all her strength. Once inside, she pointed the slime blaster into the gloom and walked slowly down a spiral staircase.

Now you may think that Barry Bigtime's dungeons would be similar to those found in a textbook about the olden days. Exposed bricks, chains and spooky stuff hanging from the ceiling, etc. What Jamie found instead was very different.

The 'dungeon' had bright blue carpets, lime green walls and was filled with beanbags. The room was divided into small sections by brightly coloured panels. In each section there was a desk and a computer. At each computer was a boy.

They seemed to be playing video games and having a lovely time. Were these boys friends or foes? Were they part of Barry's **SECRET ARMY** or something?

Wait, was that Proudy from Baezone? It was. Sure enough, all the boys seemed like they were from the party, except they all looked . . . different. They were so absorbed by the computers they hardly seemed to notice her.

Suddenly, Jamie let out a cry. Something jumped on to her backpack and scrabbled up her shoulders. Something **SLIMY LIKE A SLUG** was crawling into her ear!

Several of the boys spun around and fixed their eyes on her. She fell to the ground and grabbed hold of the attacker, pulling it off her. Then she gasped at a very friendly face. It was **BUTTONS** the pug!

If this was a film (and who knows, someday this might be) they would be playing emotional reunion music right now. Buttons would jump into Jamie's arms, she'd swing the pug around, and it would be a real **TEAR-JERKING** moment for everyone.

In reality, Jamie was still in a pile on the floor as Buttons licked her ear. She got to her feet and picked up her favourite good boy, looking over his little body to make sure he hadn't been hurt by his trip into the Boyband Generator. She looked at his squashed little face when she noticed something wasn't quite right. Buttons's eyes were completely crossed.

Before she could secure Buttons under her arm, he wriggled out of her grasp and scampered ahead, yapping. Jamie frowned. Buttons' tail was missing! She ran after the dog, but then stopped and gasped.

Sitting on a cluster of beanbags were BNA. Her chest was about to explode with excitement. How many times had she imagined being stuck in a lift with

BNA so she could ask them all the questions in the world? Now here they were trapped in a dungeon. Part of her wanted to pull up a beanbag and talk about a livestream from two years ago, but she soon remembered the mission when she saw Scott's face.

'Have you come to feed us to the bear?' asked Beck, whose voice croaked like a sad old frog's.

'Wait, aren't you the girl from the party?' asked Scott, looking stern.

Scott recognises me. Her brain was turning to ice again. Was he angry with her? Did he think that she should've tried harder to stop them going to the party? Her thoughts were getting **FUZZY.** Sentences were becoming jumbled. She had to focus!

'I'm Jamie. I was the one who told you *not* to go in!' She considered an *I told you so.* 'And I'm here to rescue you.'

'Oh yeah, it's Kid Ninja!' said Beck.

Her eyes darted from Scott, to Harrison and to Beck, and she noticed that, like Buttons, every member of BNA was looking unusual.

'Rescue us? How?' asked J, who tried to get to his

feet but now had the balance of a newborn baby giraffe and **FELL OVER,** to the amusement of Harrison, whose long flowing locks were now completely gone. His egg-like head shone in the dungeon light.

'Alright, leave it out, baldy,' said J indignantly, writhing around on the beanbag like a worm.

'Wh-what's happened to you all?' asked Jamie, trying not to **SOUND RUDE.**

'We're not sure!' said Scott glumly. 'One minute we were having a nice time at Barry's party, next thing we knew we woke up here. Harrison's hair is gone, Beck speaks like a frog, J has no balance . . .'

Jamie looked at Scott with wide eyes. 'And what happened to you?' she whispered, not totally wanting to know the answer.

'They took my happiness,' said Scott.

The words broke Jamie's heart into a thousand pieces.

'I just can't feel happy any more. I can't smile even when I try my hardest. Look, this is me trying to smile,' he said. His face looked like he'd just been told dogs had gone extinct.

Jamie's determination to take down Uncle Barry and 4TheWin quinvigupled (which we are assured means multiplied by twenty-five. Use that one to **IMPRESS** your teacher and loved ones).

Jamie's fists **CLENCHED** and she leapt to her feet. 'Don't worry, guys, I have a plan.'

CLiCK, CLiCK, CLiCK.

'Do you indeed?' came a voice and a clicking of pincers. Jamie spun round and there, still wearing her spy-man glasses, stood the hulking figure of Flobster.

'Now I don't know wh—'

SPLAT!

Before Flobster could finish, Jamie blasted him in the face with a shot of **SUPER STICKY SLIME,** sending the spy-man glasses flying off his head.

SPLAT. SPLAT.

And one for luck.

SPLAT.

Flobster tried to wipe the slime from his face but it was so sticky his claws and antennae became glued there. He panicked, **STRUGGLED** and toppled on to a beanbag and into a game-playing Fenton Dog.

The other boys in the dungeon gathered around the scene, gawping at the girl who had just wasted one of their tormentors with a home-brewed slime weapon.

Jamie looked up at her **STUNNED** audience. She felt like this would be the perfect time to say something cool but annoyingly her mind had gone blank and her adrenaline was pumping.

'Are we busting out of here or what?' shouted Jamie.

'You heard her, we're getting out of here! **Move. Move. Move!'** yelled Harrison.

A cheer rose up and a stampede of boyband members charged to the dungeon staircase. Thinking quickly, Jamie grabbed the spy-man glasses from the dungeon floor, saving them from the stamping feet of a Fenton Dog, Harrison scooped up Buttons the pug and everyone bolted through the peculiar gaming dungeon and up the spiral stairs.

They soon reappeared at the dungeon entrance. The other boybands had gone berserk and were expressing their freedom through **destruction.** Suits of armour were being tipped over, and paintings were being defaced. Someone was squatting but Jamie's brain decided that her eyes needed to leave that situation. So much for a **STEALTHY ESCAPE.**

The realisation soon dawned on Jamie that her plan to 'sneak BNA out without anyone knowing' was up in flames. Then she realised the biggest oversight in her escape plan. **WHERE ON EARTH WAS GRANDMA?**

CHAPTER 32
THE GRANNY TAKEDOWN

It was the morning of the festival, and there was no time to lose. Jenners and Mel met at Daisy's house because, unless it involved scooters, Daisy's mum Chandice was the most chilled and always had **DELICIOUS** Jamaican snacks. (Also, Daisy had been lumbered with the responsibility of looking after her little cousin Erin for the day.)

They sat round the table, studying the grandma addresses Jamie had provided them with. They drew a route on an old-skool village map like they do in police films but got **CONFUSED,** so decided to just use Google Maps instead. They packed a bag full of snacks, chocolate milk and the **LARGEST PAIR** of underpants they could find.

The girls set off for **target one:** Ethel. **Weakness:** brittle bones.

Each of them had agreed to lead individual takedowns and, because of Mel's fear of old people, she wanted to get hers out of the way first. The three of them strolled up to number 9 Richmond Road and Mel knocked on the door.

A good few seconds passed before an old lady could be heard fiddling with the latch. The door opened.

Ethel had more wrinkles than Mel had realised could fit on a face. **'WHAT?'** she snapped. It was a bad start for Mel. Fierceness made her knees wobbly.

'Oh . . .' stuttered Mel, almost losing composure. 'We're from the local Brownies and we're here to warn you about the dangers of going outside today.'

'Why aren't you wearing uniforms?' said Ethel accusingly.

Mel had to think quickly. 'Erm, because it's an emergency. It'll be **extremely slippy** outside today – it's going to be a ten on the slipometer.'

'How much does the slipometer go up to?' Ethel snarled back.

'Eleven,' said Mel seriously.

'Very slippy then.' Ethel's wispy eyebrows furrowed. 'Well, I'm supposed to go to a music concert but I can't afford to break any bones! I'm on my third hip, you see. Looks like I'll have to sit this one out.'

'Great! Well, stay safe and remember, to make sure you don't slip, just . . .' Mel had really set herself a mammoth, unnecessary task of coming up with a catchy rhyme about slipping, 'just . . . don't go outside, even a bit.'

Ethel **SLAMMED** the door in their faces.

'You did so well, Mel!' said Jenners proudly. 'Good job. NEXT.'

Daisy scrawled through Ethel's name on their list of **'GRANNIES TO NEUTRALISE'.** Next was **target two: Old Fleur. Weakness:** memory.

The girls walked on, striking a deal with Daisy's little cousin Erin about her role in the next takedown. Erin eventually agreed to a cash settlement of £10 and a chocolate bar of her choice every Saturday until Christmas.

Old Fleur lived on a sweet suburban cul-de-sac with perfectly trimmed rose hedges and a welcome mat that said, *Leave your worries at the door*. Daisy rang the doorbell for a just a second too long, meaning that a dog in the house got extra-yappy. The door slowly opened to a sweet-looking old lady using a walker, telling her dog to calm down. This was Erin's cue.

'Grandma!' she said, giving her a big hug. **'I've missed you.'**

Old Fleur pushed her glasses down to the end of her nose, looked at Erin and then back up at the three girls. 'I don't have a granddaughter,' she said, slightly confused.

There was a long, **AWKWARD,** silent pause, which eventually got broken by Jenners.

'Oh, Grandma! You're so funny!' she said, and then proceeded to also hug the elderly lady. 'Remember you promised to look after Erin all day today?'

'Did I? But I'm supposed to be going to the World Musical Concert today?'

'No, Grandma, that's next weekend,' said Jenners with a laugh. 'We'll be back to collect her tomorrow. Have fun, you two!'

By this point Old Fleur thought that

the company was a nice surprise. She shrugged and off they went to spend some pretend quality time together.

As they left Old Fleur's, a message popped up in the group chat from Jamie. She'd successfully infiltrated Barry's mansion! The girls gave a **YELP OF EXCITEMENT.** So far everything was going like clockwork.

Targets three and four: Pam and Olivia. Weakness: lax security.

The final plan was Jenners's and the most daring of all.

'Right, I've done my research,' said Jenners ominously. 'Got a few pennies, has Olivia. Made her money during the dotcom boom, bought internet. com and sold it for £4 million. Has an exotic pet tortoise called Tonga and three top-of-the-range mobility scooters in that garage. Pam's always over at Olivia's. Some say it's for granny yoga. Some say she just eats all of Olivia's expensive biscuits.'

Daisy laughed. **'Let's do this.'**

Olivia lived in the rich part of town three doors down from Tobias Merryweather's house. The front garden was huge and beautiful. Mel and Jenners hid in a bush while Daisy knocked.

Olivia opened the door, wearing head-to-toe Lycra that clung to every inch of her granny body.

Daisy gasped at the fashion travesty and **NEARLY FAINTED.**

'Are you OK, dear?' Olivia said.

'I've lost my dog,' Daisy wailed, channelling her feelings. 'I think I saw her run into your front garden.'

Olivia called for Pam, who joined the search despite not being able to see colours since 1972.

During the search, Mel and Jenners snuck into the house. Jenners swiftly moved from room to room, changing all the clocks and moving the kitchen calendar back one day, so Pam and Olivia would assume today was Saturday, not Sunday. Meanwhile, Mel found the keys to the mobility scooters in a biscuit tin and pocketed them. Even if Pam and Olivia worked out the day, they wouldn't be able to get anywhere without a scooter.

As Daisy faked a phone call about her dog having been found and thanked Pam and Olivia, Mel pressed the button on the keys which slowly opened the automatic garage door. If this part was in the movie, it would be in **SLOW MOTION** and would definitely make the trailer.

Daisy joined the others, they removed the chargers from the wall and drove out of the garage, but paused briefly to close the door, because they weren't savages. The girls couldn't believe how smoothly the Granny Takedown had gone. 'I'm gonna email the secret service to ask for work experience when I get home,' Jenners said. **'I'd make a great spy.'**

Next stop: the **WORLD MUSIC FESTIVAL.**

CHAPTER 33
THE MARSHMALLOW ROOM

'And we caught this little creature relieving himself in the corridors,' said Slottapuss, holding Fabian from The Fenton Dogz up by his collar as his legs dangled and kicked out underneath him. The boy's **THRASHING** was making it difficult for Slottapuss to keep his footing on the bouncy floor of the marshmallow room.

Barry had his fingers pressed to his temples and his eyes shut, looking like he was about to push a nuclear **EXPLOSION** out of his bottom. Fifteen minutes ago his brain had been steadily pumping out happiness chemicals as he was about to set off to the World Music Festival with 4TheWin and put on the **SHOW OF A LIFETIME** that would pay his debts and allow him to finally build the rollercoaster of his dreams. Now he was dealing with a boyband riot in his very own mansion. He'd had to take himself to the marshmallow room to try to remain calm.

'How did they escape?' growled Barry.

'We're investigating, boss. Reports say a young female intruder smuggled herself in forty-five minutes ago. She won't be hard to find. We'll be sure to bring her to you.'

'How many have escaped?' seethed Barry, rhythmically bouncing.

'None so far, boss,' said Slottapuss cheerfully. 'The perimeter is fully sealed. The fences have been electrified. We just thought we'd let them run around the grounds, tire themselves out and then we'll pop them back in the dungeon. Sound good?'

'Back in the dungeon?' yelled Barry, bouncing with more anger. **'Feed them to the sharks!** All of them! Starting with this foul creature!' he shouted, pointing at Fabian. 'Fetch me a buggy. I'll feed BNA to the sharks myself. I want this dealt with before we get to the World Music Festival. I don't want any of these slugs **spoiling our big day!** Also fetch 4TheWin. It would be good for them to see what happens when you cross Barry Bigtime.'

Slottapuss nodded and dragged Fabian away, kicking and screaming. Barry fell backwards on the cushioned floor of the marshmallow room. He closed his eyes and massaged his temples. Nothing could make this day any more annoying.

'Glennykins!'

His eyes **SNAPPED OPEN.** Surely not. There was only one person in the world who still called him Glen. Maybe if he didn't look at it, it would go away.

'Isn't this room a delight! Oooh, here comes your mother!'

Barry sat up and there, lolloping towards him with outstretched arms and puckered lips, was Grandma.

'No! No! No! Not today, Mother! You were told, I can't do birthday time today! **I'm busy!'**

Grandma's face instantly changed. 'Thirty minutes a year, that's all I ask of you!' she yelled. 'I guess I would be a fool to expect a card or maybe a thoughtful gift?'

Barry's eyes darted around the marshmallow room, the one room devoid of any items he could masquerade as a birthday gift.

'No, I didn't think so,' said Grandma, looking hurt.

'If you can't be bothered to get your mum a card or a present then the least you can do is be a good boy and have lunch with your mother and your niece!'

BARRY EXPLODED. 'I'm out here trying to make something of myself, Mother! I'm spending every minute of my day trying to make the biggest boyband in the world! Something you never believed in anyway and – wait, what niece?' Barry's eyes **NARROWED.**

'What niece? My goodness, Glen, you never cease to amaze me. *Your* niece, Sarah's daughter Jamie. Incredibly intelligent, red hair and freckles, loves her music – you two were very similar at that age, you know . . .'

'What music does she like?' hissed Barry in that cold way we all know means bad news.

'Oh, she likes all sorts but there's one band she loves . . .'

'And which band is that?' said Barry, walking towards Grandma, which would have seemed threatening if it wasn't for the bounciness of the floor.

'Oh . . . I don't know the name . . .'

'Think, old woman!' yelled Barry grabbing his mother by the shoulders.

'I don't know, Barry! BN something?'

'BNA?'

'That's the one!'

'And she was here with you?'

'She WAS here, but then she popped off with a disagreeable tum.'

Barry stormed out of the marshmallow room. His golf cart was parked outside. Had his own niece freed the boybands? How had she known that BNA were here? Wandering off and messing up his stuff, just like her mother used to.

He **SLAMMED** his foot down and accelerated along the corridor.

'Don't you go anywhere!' yelled Grandma. 'You owe me my thirty minutes!'

She climbed on her scooter and gave chase.

CHAPTER 34
THE LAST STAND OF THE BOYBANDS

Jamie, BNA and the other boybands were **SURROUNDED.** Barry's staff, truth-twisters and gruesome minions were closing in. Some of the boys who had tried to jump the chateau fence had suffered nasty electric shocks and the only exit Jamie knew of was behind a wall of enemies. The last drops of extra-sticky slime **GURGLED AND BUBBLED** pathetically from the barrel of her slime blaster. She looked behind her, hoping for an escape route.

Above the scared faces of the boybands towered the trees of the surrounding woods, the red-brick tiles of the mansion garages and the hulking blue steel of the Union Jack tour bus. There was nowhere left to run. Slottapuss pushed to the front, glaring at Jamie.

'Say, Henrik. Why does this girl look so familiar?'

'Doesn't look familiar to me, Slotty,' said Henrik.

'Yeah she does, wasn't she the one—'

Suddenly there was an explosion of pink as Barry **PLOUGHED** through his own staff in an absurd-looking golf buggy. He stepped out and locked eyes with his niece. Jamie hadn't seen her uncle Barry in real life for years. He looked even more **FRIGHTENING** in the flesh. After everything that had happened, they were finally face to face.

Jamie's mouth dropped open as Barry's passengers stepped out. Tobias, Benji, Filbert and Wilbur were in tow, each with a matching **SMUG GRIN.** Tobias was wearing comically large sunglasses, a spiked leather jacket and a scarf with twinkling LED lights. He looked 100 per cent like a baddie.

'Well, well, well, if it isn't **LAME-Y McFLAIR** and the BN-Lame-Ohs,' said Tobias as his friends laughed loudly, yelling stuff like 'Savage!' 'Owned' and **'Sick burn'.**

'Looks like the end of the road for your pathetic careers. There are new superstars in town!' Tobias pulled his sunglasses down his nose, looking Jamie dead in the eyes, and wiggled his eyebrows.

'You're not a superstar!' shouted Jamie. 'You just stole your talent from **BETTER** boybands who had **ACTUAL** skills.'

Barry gave a big pretend yawn and looked at his watch. 'Right, then, everyone. I'm bored of all of this. We've got a festival to open. You all now have two options. Option one: you go back downstairs like good boys, you can play all the video games you like, and I will make you my personal influencers. You'll all do OK on accounts with 30,000 followers and you will be the personal human billboards of BigTimeNiceTimes Inc. How does that sound?'

Jamie could hear murmurs of: 'That sounds like a pretty good deal, actually' behind her and, to her horror, some of the other boyband members started to make their way over to Barry. To her relief, **BNA STAYED BY HER SIDE.**

'There's no way we're joining you, pal, after everything you've done!' said Harrison. Buttons, who was still in his arms, gave a yap of agreement. 'Not for all the free food and drink in the world!'

'Yeah, you can do one, mate!' shouted Beck, which would have sounded tough if it wasn't for his newfound frog voice.

'Shove your BigTime up your—' shouted J whose sentence was luckily cut short as he tried to regain his non-existent balance.

Barry opened his arms and gave a wide smile. 'Or you can go for option two: stay where you are, and Slottapuss and my team will escort you to the cancellation pool, where a terrible **snack-cident** will take place. You'll be shark poop within forty-eight hours.'

The boys looked confused.

'AKA I'LL FEED YOU TO SHARKS!' Barry yelled.

With that, every last boyband member that had been standing by Jamie and BNA's side scampered over to join Barry, Tobias and the rest of the foes. Only Jamie, Buttons and BNA remained. Jamie looked up at Scott, who had remained silent this whole time, until he took her hand in his as if accepting their fate . . .

VROOOOOM!

Steaming through the mob came Grandma on her mobility scooter: face like thunder, taking no prisoners. She screeched to a halt inches in front of Jamie.

Barry rolled his eyes. 'Mother, by my watch your thirty minutes of birthday time is now up. Take yourself and Janine home. The fact that I'm not feeding you both to sharks can be your birthday gift this year.'

Without a word, Grandma pulled a Mentos and cola grenade from Jamie's belt and threw it full pelt at Barry's head, where it connected with a **THWUNK.** The bottle exploded on impact, sending sticky brown cola all over Barry, Tobias and the surrounding hench-people, who all **SCREAMED.**

Grandma jumped off the scooter, reached into her handbag and pulled out a set of keys. She jangled them at Jamie. 'I've helped myself to a birthday present,' she said with a wink, and waddled with pace towards 4TheWin's Union Jack tour bus.

Jamie turned to see a mob led by Slottapuss, who had recovered from the grenade, charging towards her. 'Scott, carry J!' she shouted over the din.

Scott, still expressionless, obeyed and ran towards the bus with Beck under his right arm.

Jamie handed her cola and Mentos grenades to Harrison and Beck, who threw them at the charging horde.

Slottapuss was no more than ten feet away from her. Jamie drew the last weapons in her arsenal, the pistols filled with bin juice, itching powder and Grandma's perfume. She **BLASTED** him full in the face. Slottapuss was stunned to a stop. He'd never tasted anything so delicious in his entire miserable life. His long, worm-like tongue lapped up all the juicy droplets from around his muzzle. Jamie threw the pistols as far as she could and Slottapuss chased after the delights, bouldering through the other charging minions.

The bus engine sprang into life. Jamie turned, ran and jumped on with Harrison and Beck, slamming the door shut. Buttons barked by their feet.

THE BUS LURCHED FORWARD and sped through the grounds, ripping up the immaculate lawns and smashing into the statues of Barry.

If Jamie thought Grandma's scooter skills were terrifying, it was nothing compared to her being behind the wheel of a double-decker tour bus.

'Sick to death of it, I am, Jamie,' ranted Grandma as they burst through the mansion's gates and out on to the road. Jamie's last sight of BigTime Manor was Barry shaking his fist, **ROARING WITH RAGE,** covered in cola.

'Every year's the same. No card, no present, but at least I get my thirty minutes. This year was the final straw.' Jamie could just about hear Grandma over the **CACOPHONY OF CAR HORNS** and yells from terrified motorists and pedestrians.

'Last present I got from him was Sheamus. Eight years ago! So I thought, if he won't buy me a present, I'll help myself. I went to help myself to a tin of Marks & Andrews finest shortbread, but all there was inside was a set of keys! I'll have those then, I thought. **It's my lucky day!'**

Bizarrely, Jamie's plan could not have gone better if it had been the plan she'd actually planned. Not only had she rescued BNA, but she'd also stopped 4TheWin from getting to the festival completely. Without 4TheWin, the festival would need a new opening act. And she had the perfect replacement. **THE TRUTH.**

CHAPTER 35
THE WORLD MUSIC FESTIVAL

Usually, in the final **DRAMATIC** chapters of a story, it's all a bit of a rush for people to get where they need to be. In this story though, Jenners, Daisy and Mel had arrived at the festival forty-five minutes **EARLY.** Jamie had forwarded the e-tickets from Grandma's phone the day before, so the girls were free to enjoy the festival at their leisure before Jamie arrived.

Hundreds of stands surrounded the park, each representing a different nation of the world. At the Indian stand there was a cookery class in action, the smells of spices making everybody's noses happy while kids ran around throwing coloured paint powder into the air.

A little further down stood the South Korean stand, where an upcoming K-pop act were playing a surprise set while an audience gathered for a traditional hanbok fashion show. Nearby, an area had been cordoned off for the group stages of the **ULTIMATE FRISBEE WORLD CUP,** where France were taking on the USA. There was also a hot dog making contest, where Germany had set a new world record for the most hot dogs made in a minute.

Jenners wandered to the Guess the Weight of the Haggis competition and scribbled down her entry while Daisy and Mel enjoyed traditional shortbread.

4TheWin were due to be the opening main stage act, which was ideal for Jenners, as she had to be home by 9 p.m. to meet the conditions of her electronic tag. It was less ideal for Jamie who was nowhere to be seen. She'd not replied to any messages since she'd entered the chateau.

'Should we ring her?' asked Daisy.

'What if she's still trying to stealthily escape with BNA? She might get spotted,' said Jenners.

'Does anyone else feel bad that we've made all of Jamie's grandma's friends miss her birthday trip? I hope it doesn't make her sad,' said Mel.

Nobody else felt bad because nobody else had

thought of this. But their contemplation was interrupted. 'LOOK!' shouted Daisy.

Weaving through the international food vans was 4TheWin's Union Jack tour bus. The bus **SCREECHED** to a halt in a space that wasn't quite big enough for it, and a girl with instantly recognisable red hair bundled out of the door.

'JAMIE!' the girls yelled in unison and rushed into a solid ten-out-of-ten group hug. Jenners broke the hug to fistbump Grandma, who'd followed Jamie out of the bus.

'Oh, GROTSACKS!' shouted Grandma. 'I forgot to pick up Pam, Olivia, Ethel and Old Fleur! I got carried away with stealing the bus!'

Jenners put an arm around Grandma. 'They'd have only slowed you down,' she said hurriedly.

'You're right. **Ethel wouldn't survive the mosh pits.** She's got bones like twiglets that woman. Right, I've been dying for a wee since I covered my idiot son in fizzy pop. I'm off to find the posh loos!' With that, the old lady left the eleven-year-olds by the stolen tour bus.

'You stopped replying in the chat, we thought you were a goner!' said Mel, giving her an extra squeeze. Buttons got excitable as he sensed feelings.

'I almost was,' Jamie said. 'I'll explain later. We need to move quickly – I need you to meet some people . . .'

The next few seconds happened in slow motion, as Scott, Harrison, Beck and J stepped down on to the grass.

Daisy, Mel and Jenners had played this moment out in their heads thousands of times, meticulously rehearsing what their first words to their **ULTIMATE HEROES** would be. However, none of their practised scenarios featured Jamie's grandma driving a bus or Harrison with a bald egg head. The girls were overwhelmed, overexcited, nervous, shocked, happy, hungry and confused. They all spoke at the same time.

'Great . . . to . . . finally—' began Jenners.

Daisy remained cool but spoke over Jenners. 'I've seen you play twenty-one times—'

Mel full on panicked and burst into her favourite BNA song, '*You don't need me, I'm not good for youuuu . . .*' **AND THEN BURPED.**

There was a moment of awkward silence. Which was made slightly more awkward by J toppling to the ground for no real reason.

Scott summoned as much happiness as he could, which was none. 'It's nice to meet you,' he said with **MAXIMUM GLUMNESS.**

'Barry stole Scott's happiness,' Jamie said to the furious girls.

Mel was so cross, she thought she could hear her own brain whirring with rage, a sound which got **LOUDER** and **LOUDER** until she could barely hear herself think. She looked around to see if anyone else could hear her brain too and then cast her eyes upwards.

Flying low above the World Music Festival grounds was a helicopter shaped like Barry's giant evil head or, as he liked to call it, the **ROFLCOPTER.** He flew over the festival like an evil Santa about to deliver four presents nobody wanted.

'4TheWin,' cursed Jamie, looking at Jenners, who had reached full Jenzilla. 'They're going to make their slot. Mel, do you have the pants?'

Mel proudly brandished the pants and whirled

them around on her index finger.

'Right. Jenners and Daisy, know what you're doing?'

'Affirmative!' replied Jenners, saluting. 'As soon as 4TheWin take the stage, make sure the cameras are on Mel.'

'Correct. How are you going to do it?' asked Jamie.

'I've got something up my sleeve,' said Jenners with a grin.

'Mel, when you see yourself on the big screen, what do you do?'

'Throw pants! Throw pants!' chanted Mel.

'Perfect. I think I know just the boys who can help you get to the front of the stage.' Jamie smiled at BNA.

'It's payback time,' said Harrison, head gleaming.

A loud SCREEECH rang out from the gigantic speakers at the main stage before a *tap, tap* and, 'Ladies and gentlemen, my name is Will Kelly – you may know me from *The Big Time*!' He waited. A small cheer rang out. 'This is your ten-minute warning. We will be live across fifty-four countries from the World Music Festival with our opening act 4TheWin in ten minutes!

Please finish your activities and head towards the stage. Ten minutes, I repeat, ten minutes!'

NO WORDS WERE NEEDED, just a few too many nods. Everyone knew what they had to do and disappeared in their different directions.

Daisy and Jenners bolted towards the AV rig. (At festivals there is a raised platform where the camera operators control what you see on the big screens and what people at home see on their televisions.) The girls slipped past security and climbed up a ladder on to the platform.

'That looks like a cool camera!' said Daisy to a confused but friendly cameraman.

'Probably not as good as my phone camera, though, right?' added Jenners.

The skinny man laughed, assuming they must be someone important's daughters, otherwise why would there be children running around the AV rig? 'Oh, it's a little bit better than that old thing, I'm afraid. In a different league. **More expensive too!'**

'Oh, is it, how come? What can it do?' Daisy asked, faking **GENUINE INTEREST.**

'Well, for starters it's better quality and can zoom much further in so we get all the action!' the man said, **SLIGHTLY DISGRUNTLED.** Every kid with a phone thought they were a camera expert these days.

'FIVE MINUTES UNTIL SHOWTIME!' came Will Kelly's booming voice from the stage.

Meanwhile, Mel, Jamie and BNA were battling the crowds, with Buttons in Scott's arms and J on Harrison's back. The further they went, the more compact the bodies became. Eventually they **SQUEEZED** to the front, right by the stage.

Mel pulled out the pants and a carton of chocolate milk.

'IT'S ALMOST SHOWTIME!' came Will Kelly's booming voice. '4THEWIN WILL BE HERE IN FIVE . . . FOUR . . . THREE . . . TWO . . . ONE . . .'

A huge graphic launched on the screens either side of the main stage. It was Barry's face looking extra evil in 4K.

'LIVE . . . ACROSS THE GLOBE . . . FROM THE ONE AND ONLY WORLD MUSIC FESTIVAL, PLEASE WELCOME . . . 4THEWIN!'

The crowd **ERUPTED WITH ALMIGHTY CHEERS** and applause that rippled back from the front of the stage. No one could argue that this audience wasn't excited to see 4TheWin.

Tobias Merryweather led the group on stage in a pair of leather trousers that he would have been the first person to make fun of just a few weeks earlier. Next came Filbert, donning a leather waistcoat, followed by Benji wearing a leather backpack and finally Wilbur, who was wearing a leather onesie. Why were they all wearing leather? **NO ONE WAS SURE.**

They launched into 'Not Who You Say You Are', the song rumoured to become their second single. There was no denying that, despite the restrictive leather waistcoat, Filbert's opening verse was on point.

'OK, Mel, we need to get you as high as possible to give Daisy and Jenners the signal,' Jamie said. 'I'll douse the pants.'

Jamie realised dousing pants in chocolate milk in a crowd was **VERY IMPRACTICAL.** It splashed on to some of the annoyed people around her.

'Hey! Don't I recognise you from somewhere?' said a man in head-to-toe 4TheWin merchandise, pointing at Scott.

At the AV rig, the cameraman was starting to lose patience with Daisy and Jenners. 'Girls, the show's started. **I need you both to leave.**'

Daisy looked over to Jenners, who was squinting into the crowd. There was no sign of Mel, but it was now or never. 'NOW!' Daisy shouted.

Quick as a flash, Jenners locked the cameraman into a full nelson wrestling hold. Daisy grabbed the handles of the camera, desperately searching for Mel.

'What the— No! You can't . . . Give me that back,' yelled the cameraman in disbelief as he tried to escape Jenners's hold, to no avail.

Then, Daisy spotted her. Sitting on Harrison's shoulders was Beck, and sitting on *his* shoulders was Mel, **FRANTICALLY WAVING** her yellow sun hat while holding something brown and dripping. Daisy zoomed in, projecting Mel on to the big screens by the stage.

Mel spotted herself. She knew this was her moment to shine, but there was a problem. Some of the

4TheWin fans had recognised BNA from their embarrassment on *The Big Time* and spotted the chocolate-milk-covered underpants. They'd sussed the plan and begun to shake the BNA tower to try to topple Mel. She couldn't get **A CLEAR SHOT.**

Things on the AV platform were getting chaotic. The cameraman wasn't going down without a fight.

'What's taking Mel so long?' shouted Jenners. 'This guy is so wriggly!'

The man slipped out of the hold and made a grab for Daisy. Jenners leapt forward and grabbed his leg, sending the man crashing into a desk, pressing about fourteen buttons at the same time.

There was a gasp as the giant festival screens flickered before throwing a new image on the display.

'My, these arms are really something, I suppose you work out *every day*?' a voice boomed across the festival grounds, hijacking 4TheWin's set.

There, backstage, being held in the arms of a younger gentleman security guard, was Grandma. Completely oblivious to the fact that she was now being broadcast to not only the festival but fifty-four countries around the world, Grandma giggled and blushed, saying things like, 'Oh, you're so silly,' and, **'Not at my age, dear.'**

No one wanted to watch this. Least of all Jamie, who was trying to fend off 4TheWin fans.

The crowd began booing. Slowly at first but then ever increasing in volume and ferocity until the whole arena echoed with **DISGRUNTLEMENT.**

Barry Bigtime, who up until this point had been smugly watching from the side of the stage, poked his head out to see his mother's face on-screen and the booing crowd. He screamed. Then he looked at

4TheWin and his purple face paled. 'NOOOO!' He knew what could come next.

4TheWin, who couldn't see the screens facing out to the crowd, were desperately trying to figure out what was happening. **WHY WERE THEY BEING BOOED?** Were they out of tune? Was Wilbur's backflip not to its usual standard?

'I knew it was too much leather,' said Benji, panicking.

But then came a cheer from the crowd as the screens flicked back to Tobias. Smiles returned to the boys' faces.

Barry breathed a sigh of relief.

Until all of a sudden, something soaked in a wet brown liquid sprung from nowhere and hit Tobias in the face with a big wet **PLAP.**

The boys looked at Tobias, then one another, their song clattering to an awkward stop.

This was the most Jamie had ever smiled. She was always proud of her friends but never more so than in this moment. Some of the audience were booing, but most were laughing. Wilbur and Benji ran to help Tobias.

Jamie turned to BNA. 'Now's your chance!' she said. **THE PLAN HAD GONE PERFECTLY.**

Until a large, green tentacle flopped out of Tobias's sleeve . . .

CHAPTER 36

PLEASE. REMAIN. CALM.

One tentacle was followed by another, then another, and then the amount of tentacles **QUINVIGUPLED.** (That's times twenty-five, remember?)

Tobias had been so **HUMILIATED** that his octopus form was growing bigger than ever. Wilbur's body parts began expanding at an astonishing rate. Benji's body stretched and swelled and morphed into a long black snake the size of a car, without a single floppy hair out of place. Filbert had become the egg and was ready to hatch.

Scott, Beck, Harrison, J, Mel and Jamie stood open-mouthed, unable to move. These did not look like pranks. She knew that 4TheWin had stolen BNA's talents and she knew that Barry's machine was awful, but this was the **STUFF OF NIGHTMARES.**

The audience, still convinced this was part of the

show, ooohed and ahhed, until one of Tobias's tentacles wrapped around a technician and dropped them, kicking and screaming, into his mouth with a **GULP.**

The crowd gasped. They finally understood. Then they screamed and began to flee in all directions, while security guards tried to make their way to the front.

Jamie turned to the others, eyes wide. 'Quick! Under there!' She pointed towards the stage. They clambered over the barriers, lifted up the curtain underneath the stage and piled in.

'WHAT IN BEJEBUS'S NAME IS HAPPENING!?' croaked Beck.

'Shhh!' replied Jamie, who had no acceptable answer to that question but knew that making noise was unwise. **HER BRAIN WAS IN OVERDRIVE:** *think, think, think.*

The stage rattled above them as a squawking Filbert hatched from his egg, slamming his giant, hairless chicken feet just metres away from them. Then came the *HISSS* of the gigantic, floppy-haired snake. It had its eyes fixed on an ice-cream van and glided through the mayhem of screams and shouts of the panicking crowd, its tail thrashing back and forth into people and Portaloos alike.

'What do we do?' said J, near tears. Beck and Harrison lay face down on the ground, desperately hoping this was the end of a weird dream or an elaborate, high-budget YouTube prank.

'Oh my . . .' said Scott, who for the first time sounded **SHOCKED** rather than sad.

Jamie felt awful. It was her plan that had turned Tobias, Benji, Filbert and Wilbur into monsters. 'We can't just hide here, we need to do something!'

Further out in the crowd, Benji had moved on to his next treat. He drove his fangs into the 4TheWin tour bus, feasting on the petrol inside.

TERRIFIED SCREAMS came from all directions as a stampede began, the crowds clambering over each other in a desperate race to avoid becoming a snack for the unimaginable beasts. Cars were spinning in the mud, food trucks tipped over and an array of belongings lay scattered across the grass.

Jamie didn't want to watch but it was not her style to bury her head in the sand. *Where are Daisy and Jenners? And what about—*

'MEL!!!'

There, being hoisted off the ground in the tight clasp of Tobias's tentacles, was Mel.

Jamie ran out, arms waving. 'HEY! HEY! OVER HERE, TOBIAS! THIS WAS MY PLAN!

I'M THE ONE YOU WANT.'

Most of Tobias's tentacles were firmly gripped on Mel, but he rotated his slimy green octopus head to look Jamie directly in the eye.

Mel used Jamie's distraction to wriggle free from Tobias's grip and crashed to the floor with a **THUMP,** covered in stinky, snotty goo.

Nearby, Scott and Harrison were desperately trying to fend off the hairless, squawking Filbert with a microphone stand, while dodging his hammering beak.

'GET UP HERE, BOYS! WE NEED YOU TOO!' shouted Harrison.

Mel, still sprawled on the floor, started searching through her bag. She had an idea. 'This better work,' she prayed and gave the honker horn a squeeze.

EYORRRE.

Tobias turned his head and let out a rumbling roar. He lifted a tentacle high and then swung it downwards, taking Jamie off her feet and knocking her out cold.

'JAMIE!' shouted Mel, sliding around on her hands and knees. She dragged herself over to Jamie's motionless body. '*No*. It was my fault again,' she sobbed.

'Get up, Mel!'

It was Daisy, followed by Jenners, who ran over to Jamie and scooped her up in her arms.

'RUN!' Daisy pulled Mel to her feet, narrowly missing another tentacle swipe that crashed through the stage. 'Look!'

On what remained of the stage, pinned up against the speakers on one side, were Harrison, J and Beck, standing protectively over Scott, who was slumped on the floor. Filbert gave a triumphant **'SQUAWKKK'** and opened his wings out wide.

With Jamie in her arms and Mel and Daisy close behind, Jenners ran towards Filbert and bashed into him with her shoulder. She bounced straight off and spilled Jamie, who awoke confused and just in time to see the giant face of Filbert staring down at the group.

Benji had slithered to their side, spitting like a cobra. Wilbur, who at this point was just giant hands and feet, loomed into view as Tobias's flailing tentacles towered over them all.

Jamie suddenly felt **VERY PEACEFUL.** The screams

and sounds of the festival started to fade away. The monsters stopped being scary and she felt lucky that her last few seconds would be spent with her three best friends and the band that had **MADE THEIR FRIENDSHIP SO STRONG.**

In that moment, deep down the girls felt sorry for their **MONSTROUS RIVALS.** They'd been annoying boys but they didn't deserve this. They never chose to be monsters. Barry had used them just like everyone else. Daisy, Mel and Jamie held hands with Jenners, as Scott, Beck, J and Harrison held them too, with enough time for one final group hug, the one that they'd always dreamed of.

'I remember in reception, I fell over in the playground and Wilbur, you helped me up.'

IT WAS MEL. She stood up in front of the group. Filbert turned to lock eyes with her.

'And Filbert, in Year 3 when I got lost on my first day, you showed me where to go.'

Mel walked fearlessly over to a microphone lying on the floor and picked it up. 'And Tobias, remember when you shared my homework and then afterwards you gave me your lunch to say thank you? **THAT WAS GOOD OF YOU.** And Benji, in Year 4, Jenners told me she had a crush on you.'

Mel's voice **BOOMED** across what was left of the festival. Wilbur stood still, his head and snout rotating to look back at the stage. Benji's face started to become less reptilious and a lot more recognisable.

For once, Jenners did not argue. 'Keep going, Mel!'

'And Benji. Remember when you told me how to upgrade my coops into barns on *FarmVillage*? That was so nice of you!'

Benji's serpent body began to **SHRINK.**

Jamie jumped up and joined Mel. 'None of this is your fault. Barry didn't tell you this would happen!'

The girls continued to say genuinely nice things about the boys and soon all four of the creatures began to change. The monsters that had caused so much terror now twisted and turned, flailed and writhed until they shrunk down into four unconscious boys.

Mel approached Filbert and put her fingers on to his wrist like she'd seen on medical TV shows. **'They need help!'**

Jenners, Jamie, Daisy and BNA quickly hoisted up one boy between two.

'There's still people in the medical tent – take them there,' Mel said, taking control.

As they arrived, **FRANTIC** medical staff laid them on the floor as the beds were already taken, and got to work. Ambulances, fire engines, police cars and a new ice-cream van screeched on to the scene.

'What has Barry done?' said Jenners, still in shock.

'BARRY!' Jamie gasped and, without looking back, sprinted as fast as her tired legs could carry her to behind the stage, with Jenners in hot pursuit.

The backstage area was the only place that remained vaguely intact. Jamie and Jenners ran past broadcast lorries full of expensive-looking screens and cables, towards rows of trailers, where the acts would have hung out before their set. The artists' names were scrawled on each door. Jamie's eyes darted from trailer to trailer.

'So you're saying you had absolutely no idea they had any – how would you say – **abnormal qualities,** sir?'

Jenners froze and grabbed Jamie. 'That's Detective

Lansdown. He's the one who arrested me and gave me my tag!' Jenners said, waggling her ankle at Jamie.

'Maybe he should get one ready for Uncle Barry,' seethed Jamie.

'Oh no, Detective, absolutely no idea,' came the voice of Barry Bigtime. 'I'd have been the first to warn you. Now we can continue this tomorrow, but I really must be off, lots of press to be dealing with. Like vultures on my time, they are.'

Jamie took a deep breath and stepped out from behind the trailer.

'He *did* know. **He did all of this!** He created these monsters in a machine in his chateau!' she shouted, pointing an accusing finger at her uncle.

'Oh, Janine,' snarled Barry, as he walked over and towered above her. 'Detective, you'll have to excuse my niece, she has a very **wild imagination.** Takes after my sister, you see.'

Jenners also stepped out from her hiding place.

'NitroJen08!?' gawped Detective Lansdown. 'What are *you* doing here?!'

'It's true!' Jenners pleaded. 'Barry knew all along, he

threw a party and made 4TheWin in his basement.'

Barry laughed. **'Kids, eh?** They watch too many conspiracy theories on YouTube these days. Anyway, I'm a very busy man, Detective. Must be getting on.'

'Yes, girls, unless you have any proof of what you're saying then I suggest you run along home,' said the detective firmly.

Ksshht! 'Slotty, dear, start up the copter, will you,' said Barry into a walkie-talkie. 'Detective, I'll be happy to assist you further in your enquiries at a later date; you know where to find me.'

'That will be all, Mr Bigtime, sir,' said Lansdown.

Barry walked over to Jamie, who was fuming. 'Goodbye, darling niece.' He brought his face close to her ear and said quietly but coldly, 'You will pay dearly for this. I will tear down your house, just like I did your grandma's. **I'll take everything you own,** just like I did to your mother. I will make sure you, your friends and anyone you've ever cared about are miserable for the rest of their lives and there will be nothing you can do to stop that now, because I am Barry Bigtime.' He kissed her on the forehead and ruffled her hair.

'Thank you, Detective! I'll be sure to slip you an invite to our next party!' With that, Barry began to leave for the Roflcopter.

JAMIE SEETHED. This couldn't be happening. After everything he'd done, Barry was going to get away with it. Just like he'd done with everything else. She looked at the detective helplessly. She felt like warning him against going to any party Barry would throw. She thought of every horror she'd seen at the last party through the spy-man glasses. She—

'WAIT!' Jamie shouted.

She plunged into her BNA rucksack.

Detective Lansdown frowned. 'Girls, you're in danger of wasting police time.'

'I have something, sir. Cold, hard proof.'

From the depths of her bag, Jamie **TRIUMPHANTLY** withdrew the spy-man glasses she'd blasted off Flobster's head. She quickly synced them to her tablet.

Detective Lansdown's mouth remained fully agape as Jamie scrolled through the footage of her approaching Barry's mansion, speaking to BNA, Buttons's wobbly mansion tour, the Boyband Generator and to the disgusting lobster placing the glasses on his own head.

Lansdown looked stunned. 'MR BIGTIME! GET BACK HERE AND **EXPLAIN THIS!'**

Barry paused, looked over his shoulder and began to sprint to the Roflcopter.

'No!' Jamie led the charge and sprinted after Barry, who shot left at the end of the line of trailers. There were only twenty metres between him and the helicopter, **BLADES ALREADY SPINNING.**

But as he dashed around the corner he was forced to a stop. Skidding across his path came a golf buggy driven by Grandma.

'Glennykins!' cooed Grandma. 'Since you're here, I believe I still have a few minutes left of my birthday time! Mind if we take them now?' she shouted, making herself heard over the helicopter.

'A LITTLE HELP, BOYS!' yelled Barry, blood pulsing through the veins on his head.

With Barry blocked by the golf cart, Jamie and Jenners caught up and made a grab for him.

At the same time, Flobster sprang from the helicopter and grabbed Grandma around the neck,

SNAPPING FEROCIOUSLY with his other pincer. Henrik stood behind him in the Roflcopter, one paw outstretched, ready to help Barry on board.

'I'd stay back if I were you, young ladies,' shouted Flobster. 'If you want your grandma to keep her limbs, I'd suggest you be good little girls and let Mr Bigtime go.'

'Oh, let go of her, Flobster. There's no need for that!' shouted Henrik.

'Oh, shut up, Henrik, **you're pathetic.**' Flobster swiped his claw at the bear, which cut Henrik right across the face.

'OK, OK, OK . . .' The girls raised their hands up in front of them and took some slow steps backwards. **'Just don't hurt Grandma,'** Jamie yelled.

'You can have thirty-one minutes next year, Mother. Have a good birthday.' Barry stepped up into the chopper with help from Henrik.

Flobster kept his beady gaze on Jamie as he slowly released his grip on Grandma and leapt aboard. As he did, Barry began to close the helicopter door and pushed Henrik, who fell out and hit the floor with an almighty **THUD.**

'Sorry, bear, we need to lose a few pounds,' Barry cackled as the helicopter began to rise.

Barry shouted something else evil and menacing as his giant head lifted into the air, but thankfully no one heard it because it was drowned out by the noise of take-off. Henrik lay on the grass, covering his eyes from the swirling wind and dust.

Jamie hugged Grandma harder than she ever had. As Barry's **GINORMOUS HEAD** flew off, Grandma tutted. 'Goodness me, he might be my son but he is quite the piece of work, isn't he? Right, which way is the motorway?'

CHAPTER 37
ONE, TWO, THREE, PULL

ONE MONTH LATER

It was 9.30 a.m. on Saturday morning when Jamie was awoken by the smooth sound of her new alarm clock. She mumbled sleepily, dealt with those **EYE BOGIES** and dragged herself out of her bed burrito. She hopped to the floor and pulled open the curtains, flooding the large room with winter sunlight. She stretched and tied back her messy red hair.

'Good morning, Buttons,' she said, as the pug dozed in his basket. 'Right, better check on Grandma.'

Jamie trundled down the corridor. She glanced at the pictures in the long hallway, draped in gold tinsel. There was one of Mum and her when she was a baby, Grandma on the day she won the Crudwell **OVER-70S DANCE-OFF** and, curiously, a very realistic but olden-days photo of a baboon playing the flute.

Ten minutes later, she reached the door she was looking for. Above the door was a sign: *Heavens Above Retirement Home, accidentally funded by Glen 'Barry Bigtime' Jones.*

Through the door, Jamie found Grandma and several other oldies, lying on her back while raising her hips in the air. Sheamus the pig was in the corner of the room, snuggled into an old purple dinosaur costume.

'. . . and from bridge pose, breathe in . . . and hold . . . two, three, four, raise arms high into mountain pose . . . and into downward dog. **Hold . . . and relax.**'

Jamie put her hand to her mouth to push back a giggle.

'Great class today,' said Grandma. 'Good improvements with the hip, Ethel. See you all tomorrow bright and early,' she added as she did one final lunge in her Lycra.

As the class filtered out, Jamie ran up to Grandma and gave her **A HUG,** which she immediately wished was a pre-yoga hug rather than a post-yoga one but didn't mind.

'Looking after you OK, are they, Grandma?' said Jamie, smiling.

'I'm having the time of my life, little one!' she replied. 'I lead yoga on a Saturday, we have *Mario Kart* qualifiers on the big screen in the **BRILLIANT HALL** on a Tuesday, and I bought us all VR headsets as well! I skydived into the Grand Canyon from the marshmallow room last night!'

'Let's do that tonight after dinner!' Jamie was keen for a casual Saturday evening skydive. She looked up at the menu above the reception desk, which read: *All-You-Can-Eat Fish & Chips*.

Perfect, thought Jamie, *I'll leave some room for that*. 'See you tonight, Grandma!'

Jamie wandered out of the retirement wing and down to the still quite terrifying **BARRY-HEADED OCTOPUS-LEGGED** signpost. *We really need to change that*, she thought, although it was quite helpful in finding all of the rooms. She followed the rabbit holding the carrot that pointed to the Brilliant Hall.

Sarah and Jamie had wondered whether to rename the Brilliant Hall, after the taxman had repossessed most of the 'brilliant' items to pay off Barry's remaining debts. Eventually, though, they agreed that really the hall was still brilliant, mainly because Barry wasn't in it. It also seemed much **BIGGER** without a giant revolving disco ball, a puppy claw crane game and an empty stage.

'Mum, why are you sitting in here on your laptop?' asked Jamie, who was trying to figure out why Sarah was on the floor with Buttons, her laptop balanced on the edge of a giant bowl that had once been filled with boybands and butterscotch.

'I tell you what, for a man who was at one point so rich he had a helicopter shaped like his own head, he absolutely did not put enough plug sockets in this place,' Sarah said half jokingly, half **GENUINELY ANNOYED.** 'I'm just writing an email to Detective Lansdown thanking him.'

Detective Lansdown had conducted a full investigation into Barry's grubby dealings over the last month, meaning Sarah had finally got her money back. As Barry's closest relatives, the ownership of his chateau passed to them – not that they would still call it that.

'I should also be thanking you,' said Sarah. 'You worry the life out of me, but you're **VERY BRAVE.** Because of you we have an opportunity to use this house to do something good.' She gave Jamie a hug. 'What time is everyone coming round?'

'Really soon,' replied Jamie. **'Any news about Uncle Barry?'** she added nervously.

'He's still out there somewhere,' sighed Sarah, passing Jamie a copy of the *Crudwell Gazette*, sporting the headline *Barry Big-Crimes*. Although she'd exposed Barry Bigtime for the grotsack that he was, Jamie hated that he was still oozing evil out there somewhere.

'Jamie, would you do me a favour. Go and help Henrik do the tree in the kitchen. I left him to it but you know what he's like.'

Jamie had allowed Henrik to stay with her family. They had plenty of room now, plus the world could be a cruel place for a talking bear with human ears. Besides, it was the least she could do after breaking their **PINKY PROMISE.**

When Jamie got to Henrik, he was tangled up in red, silver and gold tinsel (no one likes all three), trying to water a fake tree while listening to a Michael Dooblé playlist because he couldn't remember the correct name. He wasn't great at trees but he was excellent at **THROWING SNOWBALLS** and he was also the only person/bear who knew anything about how the Boyband Generator worked.

DING . . . DONG
DING . . . DONG
DINGDONG
DINGDONG

'Jenners!' said Jamie excitedly and slightly nervously as she ran to the front door, followed by Buttons yapping at her heels.

DING . . . DONG
DING . . . DONG

The doorbell rang again.

'Daisy!'

All the golf carts had been sold on eBay so it took Jamie a while to run to the front of the house. She opened the door and gave Jenners and Daisy a big hug. Not far behind, **CRUNCHING UP** the gravel path were two cars. *Right on time*, thought Jamie. Buttons shot out on to the drive and cocked his leg up before doing a **BIG WEE** on the one remaining Barry statue. 'Good boy!' said Jamie, patting him on the head.

The first car door opened and out stepped J, Beck, Harrison and Scott. Out of the second car followed Benji, Wilbur, Filbert and Tobias. Everyone looked a bit nervous, except Scott, who still looked sad.

'You ready for this?' asked Jamie, leading them into the house.

'Where's Mel?' asked Daisy.

'She still thinks she can capture Barry,' said Jamie,

Mel, who had a newfound confidence since **CONQUERING THE BOYBAND MONSTERS,** had joked about capturing Barry herself for weeks, even though it was reported he'd fled the country with Baezone, The Fenton Dogz and his other boybands . . .

Jamie led the group to Barry's old laboratory, whilst J, who still had no balance, clung on to Harrison's arm. Waiting there was Henrik, minus tinsel but complete with fez.

'OK then, everyone,' he said pointing at the Boyband Generator. 'According to the instructions, Tobias, Wilbur, Filbert and Benji, we need a DNA ingredient from you. **You can either pluck a hair, or spit in here – your call.'**

Henrik offered up a bowl and the four boys spat in it like an odd dentist appointment.

'Wonderful. Tobias, Wilbur, Filbert, Benji – take a seat in the mouth and make yourselves as comfortable as possible. Scott, Harrison, J and Beck, if one of you could take Buttons, find yourself a dome, attach the headgear and think happy thoughts.'

Buttons leapt into Harrison's arms and they walked over to the domes.

DING!

'Wait!' said Jamie, opening a message on her phone.

'It's Mel . . . and it looks important!' She read the message aloud. 'I've got him!! Found him trying to sneak into the chateau. Can't believe it.'

Jamie's eyes widened and her heartbeat quickened.

Excitement bubbled around the room.

YOU'VE CAPTURED BARRY!?? WHAT? HOW?

Jamie didn't need to wait long to find out, as Mel triumphantly strode into the dungeon with her struggling captive: an angry, thrashing, **MISCHIEVOUS-LOOKING GOOSE.**

'I can't believe it! I did it, I finally caught him! I used the honker horn!'

Everyone laughed and congratulated Mel on her second heroic moment of the school term.

'Are you sure reversing the Boyband Generator process is going to work?' Jamie looked at Henrik with concern.

'I've only seen it done once before. Everything went back to normal and all of the monstrous defects were completely cured,' he replied. 'As long as you remember to take the medicine every day at 6.30 a.m. . . .'

'But what about BNA? Will their talents be restored?' asked Jamie.

Henrik shrugged. 'Fingers crossed, eh?'

It was the best Jamie could hope for.

'OK.' Jamie squeezed the girls' hands tight as she looked up and met eyes with Scott, who for the first time in a while managed to smile.

'Shall we all do this together?' said Jamie.

The girls nodded and each grabbed the lever with a hand.

'After three?' said Jamie.

'On three or after three?' asked Jenners.

'One, two, three and pull, I think,' said Daisy.

'Sounds brilliant,' said Mel.

'One!'

'Two!'

'Wait . . . what *does* BNA stand for?' asked Henrik.

'Three!'

And on three they all yanked hard on the metal lever.

Let's leave our heroes there for now. As the machine **RUMBLED** and **BUZZED,** returning BNA's talents and de-monster-fying Tobias and his cronies, Jamie wondered what Barry was doing now. She remembered the words he'd whispered in her ear before the helicopter flew away and felt certain she hadn't seen the last of him.

But as she looked at her friends, family and the animals around her, she smiled. **HE WAS NO MATCH FOR THEM.**

ACKNOWLEDGEMENTS

There is not a big enough thank you that can go out to the five-star, excellent human that is our editor, Tig Wallace, and the whole team at Hachette Children's. (You all know who you are and you are brilliant!) From day one, everyone fully embraced our mad brains and never once tried to talk us out of our nonsense ideas. In truth, they encouraged them and for that we want to say a huge thank you and we love you! We're so happy that the world got to meet Jamie and the girls, Barry, Grandma, Henrik, Slottapus, Flobster . . . well maybe not Flobster, but you know.

Also thank you so much to YOU! The person reading this book! We really hope you enjoyed visiting this mad little world and fingers crossed, we shall see you on the next adventure!

Luke and Sean

LOOK OUT
FOR ANOTHER
HILARIOUS
ADVENTURE
FEATURING JAMIE
McFLAIR

COMING IN
MARCH 2022!

Photo © Ollie Ali

Luke Franks and Sean Thorne are a debut author duo. Luke is a presenter on CITV's *Scrambled*, has presented *The X Factor* online and *The Voice* online, and is a Sony Rising Star award-winner. Sean is a presenter on the Fun Kids radio show, runs a successful YouTube gaming channel with 120k subscribers, and is a Nickelodeon Kids Choice Award nominee.

Luke and Sean met at university and have been creating comedy together ever since. They live in London and often co-walk a dog called Goose.